"I'm ready to court you

"You're what?" Benjamin shook his head in disbelief. "Earlier today, you said just the opposite."

"A girl can change her mind, can't she? I *am* a girl, you know." Miriam's hands flew to her hips. "Whether you think of me that way or not."

"But maybe it's not such a good idea. Like you said, Stephen and Angie are two people who have a more stable life to offer Emma."

"But we're two people who can offer something that may be even better for her. Trust me—I want to court you about as much as you want to court me."

His head jerked at her frankness. Yet he didn't know why. Shouldn't he be getting used to her plainspokenness by now?

Only stopping to take a breath, she continued, "I realized you're right, Benjamin. Though I hate to admit it. Emma shouldn't be shuttled off to some foreign place right now to be with people she doesn't know."

He knew she was waiting for a response, but he didn't know what to say.

Cathy Liggett is an Ohio girl who never dreamed her writing journey would take her across the world and to Amish country, too. But she's learned God's plans for our lives are greater and more creative than the ones we often imagine for ourselves. That includes meeting her husband at a high school reunion and marrying three months later—nearly forty years ago. Together, they enjoy visiting kids and grandkids and spoiling their pup, Chaz.

Books by Cathy Liggett

Love Inspired

Her Secret Amish Match
Trusting Her Amish Heart
Their Unlikely Amish Courtship

Visit the Author Profile page at LoveInspired.com.

Their Unlikely Amish Courtship

CATHY LIGGETT

LOVE INSPIRED
INSPIRATIONAL ROMANCE

LOVE INSPIRED®

INSPIRATIONAL ROMANCE

ISBN-13: 978-1-335-59733-5

Their Unlikely Amish Courtship

Copyright © 2024 by Cathy Liggett

Love Inspired
22 Adelaide St. West, 41st Floor
Toronto, Ontario M5H 4E3, Canada
www.LoveInspired.com

Printed in Lithuania

MIX
Paper | Supporting responsible forestry
FSC® C021394

Weeping may endure for a night,
but joy cometh in the morning.
—*Psalm* 30:5

Ever since I was a little girl, I had a dream.

I'd like to dedicate this book along with my heart full of gratitude to my caring agent Karen Solem, who keeps making that dream come true!

I'd also like to give a special thank-you to my friend Nancy Bentz, whom I've shared life with forever, and that includes the lives of my fictional characters.

Also, much thanks to my talented hairstylist Christy Rack, who is a wealth of information about so many things, including pygmy goats.

Thanks, too, to Dan and Lisa Egan. You serve up the best food ever at our neighborhood Buck's Tavern and served up answers about restaurants too.

I am also very thankful to senior editor Melissa Endlich not only for the opportunity to write for Love Inspired but also for making my manuscripts so much better. Don't know how you do all you do!

Thank You, dear Lord, for bringing these people and so many others into my life. You always know what this girl needs!

Chapter One

The early morning June sun poured through Miriam Schrock's kitchen window. As she sat at her oak table, the beaming light illuminated the entire space around her. That alone should've made her feel perky and ready to shine. Plus, the fact that school had been out for several weeks and she'd been resting from planning lessons and correcting papers should've energized her as well. But so far there'd been nothing typical about this summer in Sugarcreek.

She took a last sip of her lukewarm tea before getting to her feet and carrying the mug over to the sink. Then slipping on her *kapp*, she was bent on taking the letter she'd written to her cousin straight out to the mailbox—before she changed her mind. Just then a knock on her screen door startled her. In the last few weeks, it had become a rare sound ever since Lizzie and Roman Byler, her next-door neighbors and her only close friends, had gone to be with the Lord.

Though she was sure the loving couple were resting in *Gott*'s arms, her heart still ached thinking of them. Misty tears began to cloud her eyes when the knock came again. Even so, through the screen she could tell her visitor was Benjamin, the Byler brother who was her own age. Right away, she swiped her eyes and padded to the front door. As she did, she thought that most *maedels* would've been smoothing their dresses and tucking their hair neatly under their *kapps*, attempting to look their best when greeting him. After all, even though he'd been living in Cincinnati for the past five years before returning to the Amish way of life, Benjamin was still considered to be one of Sugarcreek's most good-looking single men.

But Miriam didn't bother with that sort of thing. They'd barely ever been on speaking terms until just recently. As she opened the screen door, she wondered if she'd misunderstood what time she was supposed to sit with his eight-year-old niece.

"Am I late coming over to watch Emma? I thought you said after lunch."

"I did say after lunch," he answered tersely.

"Benjamin, what's going on?" She frowned at his hands. "Are those… Have you been cutting down my roses?"

Studying him, she was a bit confused. At nearly six feet tall, he had a strong presence, and his upper arms strained the fabric of his white short-sleeved shirt. His brown hair also still had the same boyish tints of gold it always had. But what she couldn't help but notice as he stood there clothed in plain, baggy black pants and suspenders were his blue eyes. In the past, they'd always shone in an inviting way when she'd see him talking to others. Since his brother and sister-in-law's tragic buggy accident, their color had turned a steelier hue. Today those eyes looked even more direct and businesslike. However, the fact that he had a bouquet of roses in his hands seemed at odds with his serious look.

"These aren't yours," he replied. "They're roses from the other side of Roman and Lizzie's…well, my house now," he added with a notably sad inflection. "I thought since Emma is still sleeping that I'd bring some over to you."

"Hmm. Are you sure they're from your house? Because

some look very similar to my roses. Pretty as they are, they'd last a lot longer in the ground than in a vase filled with water."

"You know, Miriam, if someone brings you flowers, it's traditional to be thankful, not annoyed." He rolled his eyes. "You also don't have to look so suspicious."

"And how should I look, Benjamin?" She couldn't help but huff back.

When Benjamin had first come back to Sugarcreek and moved in with Roman and Lizzie a few months ago, they'd hardly traded hellos. It wasn't until after the accident that they'd communicated a bit more. If a person could call their strained conversations communicating.

"How about looking delightedly surprised?" he questioned her.

"Oh, I'm surprised for sure and certain," she said.

He swished his free hand through the air as if wiping a blackboard clean. "Let's start over and pretend we don't know each other. May we do that?"

She shrugged. "I suppose we can try." To show her willingness, she stepped out onto the porch.

With that, he gripped the bouquet with both hands and looked down at his feet. Then he glanced up and managed to conjure a huge grin. "Hi. I'm Benjamin. Benjamin Byler." He offered a friendly nod. "You can call me Ben."

"Hello, Benjamin. I'm Miriam Schrock. And I have to think you're standing on my doorstep for a reason. It must be a big one if you're bringing me flowers. *Jah?*"

He seemed to relax slightly. "I wanted to thank you for how you've been so kind to Emma."

All at once, her heart completely softened at the mention of his orphaned niece.

The sweet girl had been a student of hers since she was

six. She'd grown from being a very shy child to becoming slightly more outgoing. But ever since Lizzie and Roman's funeral, she hadn't spoken a single word. No one was sure when she would ever speak again.

"You don't have to thank me, Benjamin. Emma's *verra* special to me," she said sincerely. "I've known her since she was a toddler—ever since your brother and Lizzie moved into your parents' house after your *maam* and *daed* went to be with the Lord. I just wish I knew what to do about…" She felt a catch in her throat.

"People say it'll take time, so we'll keep praying, Miriam." Benjamin's tone was shaky as well. "That's what we'll do. I'm sure *Gott* will have Emma talk again."

"*Jah*, I hope you're right." She offered him a tight-lipped smile.

"Anyway, *danke* again, and here you are."

He thrust the bouquet of roses toward her so suddenly, she jerked back and had to steady herself before she reached out her hand. As she took the flowers from his grasp, the floral scent was undeniable. So was the warmth that rushed to her cheeks. She'd never had a man give her flowers before.

"You're welcome, Benjamin. I'm here to help."

"*Gut* because there's something else I *verra* much need your help with, Miriam."

"Oh, are you still planning on opening your restaurant?" She remembered hearing from Lizzie that Benjamin and Roman had been working on that project together.

"I'm not sure. Things need to settle down more before I do. But what I really need right now is for you…to…to…"

He began to stutter like the one and only time when they were young *kinner* that he'd stopped over to ask for her help with schoolwork.

"*Jah*, Benjamin?"

"Miriam." He looked her straight in the eye. "I want to court you."

"Court me?"

She narrowed her eyes and stared through her wire-rimmed glasses at him, attempting to read his expression. But he stood staunchly and didn't blink, as if straining to look sure of himself. Yet beads of sweat began to dot his forehead, though the day hadn't heated up yet.

What could he possibly be up to? She shoved the bouquet back into his chest. Loose petals drifted to the ground. "Aren't we a bit old for pranks?"

"But it's not a prank. I'm serious. I want to court you." He offered her the roses again, which weren't as fresh-looking as before.

With a shake of her head, she refused them. "That's *verrickt*! You've never once given me a second look. And I already told you I'll help with Emma as long as I can. But you don't have to date me to have that happen. I may be known as Miriam *Shock*, thanks to you, but I'm not so awful that I wouldn't help a grieving child. Especially sweet Emma. Now, if you'll be on your way…" She shooed him with her hand. "I'll be over later to babysit. Right now, I have things to take care of."

Turning, she opened the screen door and started to step inside, knowing what she'd said wasn't totally true. Honestly, she didn't have much on her plate that morning. Except now she felt an even stronger urge to get the letter to her cousin Francie in the mailbox. After all, she was so very tired of being humiliated.

"Miriam, wait!"

Benjamin caught the door before Miriam could close it on him. No doubt about it, it was as strange for him to be asking her to court him as it had to be for her.

It wasn't that Miriam wasn't an attractive woman. It was easy to see *Gott* had blessed her. Her black hair shone like a coal-black purebred's as it grazed under the summer sun, complementing her ivory complexion. Her eyes were bluer than any he'd ever seen. But right now her lips were tightly pursed and her eyes glared more than they smiled. *Gott* forgive him for thinking it, but Miriam was a pill and a hard one to swallow at that. Even so, she was the perfect person to help him in his time of need.

"Miriam, please give me a minute to explain," he pleaded.

She put hands to her hips. "Benjamin Byler, I have a hard time believing you want to court me, and no one in all of Sugarcreek, Walnut Creek, Berlin, Millersburg and any other neighboring burgs are going to believe it either." She shook her head at him then seemed to take a moment to calm herself.

"Look," she finally said more softly, "I know you're grieving, and it's not like I don't feel for you. I do—even though you probably don't believe I'm capable of that. But you need to find someone else for your wife."

"I can't," he said matter-of-factly.

"Now that's not true. I'm sure you'd get plenty of interest if you'd venture into town."

A huge part of him did wish he could be asking anyone but Miriam to be his girl. But he couldn't. Because finding a lifelong mate wasn't what asking her to court him was all about.

Still, how could he explain his situation in a way that didn't hurt her feelings?

"I'm asking you, Miriam, because…well, one reason is that we're neighbors." That fact had made a whole lot more sense in his head than it had when it'd left his mouth.

Miriam quirked a brow. "That's ridiculous. You and I,

we're living proof that having houses close together doesn't mean being close at heart."

"That's true. But that's what's perfect about it," he blurted out. But seeing her mouth gape wide open, he backtracked. "What I mean is, we're both concerned about Emma, and you're right next door and know her better than anyone. After all, she was three years old when I moved away. She hardly knows me."

He could see her eyes soften some at the mention of his niece, so he continued. "If we're together, hopefully it'd be a situation that would feel more secure for Emma. And it helps me a lot too. Because, while I'm trying to take care of her, maintain the house, and figure out work, I really don't have time to establish a loving relationship with a *maedel*. That's why it'd be *gut* to be courting *you*."

Her eyes looked stunned and even slightly hurt. That wasn't at all what he'd meant to do.

"Miriam, I don't mean any of that in a bad way. I think you're a good person, that's why—"

She held up her hand to stop him.

"You're not making one ounce of sense, Benjamin. If you don't want to have a real relationship right now, then why court at all?"

"That's the thing. I have to." He handed the flowers back to her so abruptly that she was forced to take them. Then he bent over, lifted his pant leg slightly and pulled the latest letter from his oldest brother from his sock. "Stephen wrote to me."

"Your *Englischer* brother?" Miriam's brows peaked. "I remember seeing him and his wife at Roman and Lizzie's funeral. But I don't understand. Are you saying he wrote to you about courting?"

He nodded. "In a roundabout way."

Her forehead wrinkled and then she shook her head, as if ready to dismiss him and the nonsensical conversation. He knew he'd better be quick to explain, or she might shut the door on him again.

"He wants to take Emma away to live with him and Angie in Boston."

"What? All the way to Massachusetts?" Instantly, Miriam laid the flowers on an entry table inside her front door and came outside again, the screen door slamming shut behind her. "But why? I remember Lizzie telling me Stephen and Angie are workaholics. That they've never even stopped working long enough to consider having their own *kinner.*"

"Well, I guess that's changed." He waved the thin piece of stationery, which felt hefty in his hand. "Stephen's letter says that they're both going overseas for work for a while. Once they're finished with that project, they plan to come get Emma and raise her up East. That way Emma will be sure to have two caretakers who have steady incomes." He paused, feeling his ire rise. "Stephen didn't mince words about saying those are both things he doesn't think I can provide."

Currently, his brother was correct. Even so, in Benjamin's heart, nothing felt right about Stephen's solution where Emma was concerned. Mostly, he couldn't believe that's what Roman and Lizzie would want for their daughter. Wouldn't they want Emma to grow up in the Amish way of life until she got to an age where she could decide for herself whether to be baptized or not? That's what Stephen had gotten to do.

At sixteen, his older brother moved to Cleveland and began working at their *Englischer* uncle's company. From there he got his GED, then a college business degree which led to one success after another. Everything Stephen wrote home about his experiences had made Benjamin curious. So much so that at eighteen, he set out for Cincinnati, spending years there working as a cook and learning the restaurant business. Until recently when he had a yearning in his heart to return to Sugarcreek and be baptized.

But what if he'd never grown up knowing what the Amish faith and community was all about? With every part of him, he felt Emma shouldn't miss out on that.

"Ah… I think I'm beginning to understand," Miriam said, interrupting his thoughts. "You want to court me— someone you needn't be beholden to—so that Stephen will be convinced you're on the right course for your life and for Emma. Correct?" Her eyes brightened as if she'd solved a puzzle.

"Exactly." He sighed heavily, relieved that she understood and seemed to be taking it well. Until her expression darkened.

"Well… I'm sorry, Benjamin. *Verra* sorry. But I have to say *nee*. And it's not just because the entire town will be in an uproar, disbelieving we're a couple. I'm saying it because, with Stephen and Angie, at least Emma will have two parents and a stable home like she had before. There's something to be said for that."

His heart instantly sank with regret. He'd forgotten that Miriam's father had abandoned their family when she was all of nine years old. Obviously, the sadness of that still lingered with her to some degree. Remembering, he was sorry he'd even mentioned anything to her.

"It's *oll recht*. Don't worry," he said, hoping to hide his disappointment. "I'll figure out something. In the meantime, will you still come watch Emma for me after lunch?"

"For sure. And, Benjamin?"

"*Jah?*"

"*Danke* for the roses."

"You're welcome. But you were right," he admitted. "The white ones *are* from your bushes." He was prepared for a scolding and rightfully so.

Instead, surprisingly, Miriam answered kindly. "No worries."

He offered up a smile, though it felt like a weak one.

As he walked across the lawns back to his house, he forced himself to straighten his shoulders and reminded himself to stay strong.

He wished life was simple again, and he could stroll right into the Byler home and see his brother and Lizzie smiling at each other and doting over their *dochder*. But that's not what *Gott* had chosen to happen. That's not what had come to pass. Now, Emma was his priority and anything beyond her well-being didn't matter.

Hopefully, *Gott* would show him what was best for his young niece. With each and every step back home, that's what he prayed.

Chapter Two

A few hours later, before heading next door to watch over Emma, Miriam took a moment to glance at the mailbox at the end of her driveway. The red flag on the metal box was no longer standing upright. Her letter to Francie inquiring about job opportunities in Elizabethtown, Pennsylvania, was on its way. Of course, realistically she knew no matter where she lived if she didn't change, nothing in her life would either. She couldn't expect to find happiness, a place that felt like home and perhaps even love, if she didn't learn to let down her defenses and let others in. As scary as that thought was, she'd still written the letter. She'd done what she'd promised herself she'd do. The tranquil stillness of the summery afternoon air seemed to confirm it'd been the right thing.

Why, then, was she feeling so much turmoil?

Was it the uncertainty of her future? Or—she swayed uneasily in her sneakers—was it the awkwardness of the present?

She clutched the canvas bag dangling from her shoulder as if holding it tightly could steady her as she turned her gaze and feet toward the Byler homestead. Truthfully, she knew it wasn't only thoughts of possibly moving over three hundred miles away to Elizabethtown that'd had her insides reeling all morning. Ever since Benjamin had stopped by with his preposterous proposal, her emotions had been rising and falling nonstop like a yo-yo on a short string.

Even now, as she made her way across the lawns, she kept shaking her head. At herself. And at him. It all was so ridiculous. How dare Benjamin ask to court her when he wasn't truly interested in a serious relationship? Of course, she really would have thought he was a lunatic if he had been the least bit sincere. And yet…it had been very sweet of him to go that far all for Emma's sake. In that respect, she'd almost been sorry to turn him down.

After all, regardless of dubbing her with an awful nickname she'd probably never live down, he genuinely seemed to have a thoughtful side. Along with his concern for Emma, the roses he'd brought by were proof of that. He needn't have gone to all the trouble of presenting her with a full bouquet, even if a few had been plucked from her own garden.

Suddenly, her cheeks warmed like they had earlier when she held those fragrant blooms in her hand. Many times in the past, she'd witnessed the same kind of rosy flush on her younger sister's cheeks. Especially anytime Jeremiah Lapp displayed his affection for Rebecca with a gift. To this day, the now-married couple shared a true, honest-to-goodness love. Still to this day, for good reason, Miriam worked to cast that thought aside.

Instead, as she made her way onto Benjamin's property, she turned her attention to the mare hitched to the post in front of his house.

"Hello, there, Joy," she greeted the standard bred, running her hand gingerly over its shiny coat. "Ready to take Benjamin to town?"

The horse gave her a curious look. Most likely it was because she'd never addressed the creature before even though she'd heard Lizzie and Roman talk about Joy for years. And, for sure, she'd never petted it either.

"You know I'm stalling, don't you?" The horse instantly looked away as if already dismissing her. "You're right. I can't put off seeing Benjamin any longer, can I?"

Besides, it wasn't like she'd need to be around her neighbor for very long. He'd be leaving to do his errands. That meant she could look forward to a few peaceful hours either playing, reading or even knitting with Emma. With that in mind, she resolutely strode up the porch steps. After taking in a deep, calming breath, she knocked on the screen door and waited.

Then waited some more. Still, no sound of footsteps answered her. No one called out to her. After taking time to count slowly to ten, she knocked again. Once more, silence replied.

Had she gotten the time wrong?

Or were Benjamin and Emma outside somewhere?

She started to walk away from the door to check. But then suddenly she heard Benjamin's voice. Instantly, chills ran up her arms. He was frantically shouting Emma's name.

"Emma! Where are you? Emma, please stop hiding!"

Without a moment's hesitation, she tore open the door and stepped inside. Tossing her tote on the nearest chair, she hurriedly ran to the room he was calling from.

"Benjamin, what's wrong? What's going on?"

"I can't find her, Miriam. I can't find Emma."

"You mean she's…she's lost?" Her mind wrestled to make sense of his words. Her every limb stiffened with fear.

"I don't know. I don't know," he wailed. "She was playing with her doll in her bedroom. I went in to tell her that I was going to the barn to get Joy and that you'd be here any minute. But when I got back…she…she wasn't here."

He clutched at his hair as if close to pulling it out. "Where could she have gone? I've been calling her name ever since, but she hasn't answered me."

Miriam shot him a puzzled look.

"That was stupid of me to say, I know." He shook his head. "She hasn't answered anyone about anything. But she could've come when she heard me calling her. And she hasn't."

"What if she took her doll down to the cellar?" Miriam suggested. "Then maybe she wouldn't have heard you yelling for her."

She scarcely believed what she was saying, but Benjamin seemed to embrace the idea. His eyes widened with hope before he tore out of the room.

Rushing toward the basement door, he flew down the steps. She followed closely behind him. As their feet hit the concrete floor, their voices echoed one another's as they continued to call out Emma's name. After searching behind every shelf stocked with canned goods, around stored cardboard boxes and under the bassinet Lizzie hadn't gotten to use again, they despairingly trudged back upstairs.

Standing in the living room, Miriam knew Benjamin was as overwrought as she was. Even so, she couldn't hold back her questions.

"Are you sure you looked everywhere? In all the closets?"

"Of course, I did. I checked in every closet, under the beds. Oh, I can't believe this!" His hands knotted into fists. "I watch my niece for just a few weeks, and this is what happens? This is the best I can do?"

"She can't be far. We'll find her, Benjamin." She laid a comforting hand on his forearm, but he was quick to slough it off.

"Stephen's right," he said harshly. "What was I thinking? I can't take care of a child."

"Oh, please, stop it!" She yelped at him. "We've got a little girl to find. This isn't the time to be going on about yourself."

"You're right." He straightened. "You're right," he repeated. "I'm sorry. It's just…where can she be, Miriam? She's not here. She's not at your house. And I didn't see her outside the house when I came in from the barn."

Her mind was in as much of a turmoil as Benjamin's seemed to be. She thought she'd been anxious on her walk over, but now her nervousness was spiked with fright. She closed her eyes, working to calm herself.

The Lord is my shepherd… The Lord is my shepherd…

The first few verses of Psalm 23 came to mind, just as they always had ever since she was a young girl. She'd recited the scripture plenty of times when she'd lay in bed frightened by the night's darkness in a house that was unprotected by a father. It was also a verse she depended on when hoping to be led in a right direction. Like now.

As she opened her eyes, she did feel somewhat less panicked. It must have shown in her expression.

Benjamin leaned closer. "What are you thinking?" he asked.

"I'm thinking we need to think."

"*Jah?* Like I haven't been doing just that?" he replied sharply.

"No, I mean really stop and consider everything."

He crossed his arms over his chest and frowned at her.

"Look, Benjamin, you keep asking where Emma would go, and you're right. Where would that be? She isn't *verra* daring, especially these days. I can't imagine her venturing into town. Or even sneaking down the road to her friend

Sarah Burkholder's house. If she has gone off somewhere, it's got to be someplace close. Somewhere that doesn't pose a threat to her."

"Some place like…?" Benjamin raised his arms in the air, waiting for her to fill in the blank.

She went through every scenario she could imagine. And then it hit her. "I think I know where to look!"

At least she hoped she did.

The Lord is my shepherd. Please, Lord, be our shepherd, she begged *Gott* as she hurriedly led the way out the front door.

Benjamin could tell Miriam was sure she was headed in the right direction. But as they ran between their two houses, his doubts began to outweigh his hope.

Too many nights when he'd been living an *Englischer*'s sort of life in Cincinnati, he'd watched the eleven o'clock news. At first, it had never made much sense to him that after putting in long hours at work, people ended their day with such sad, atrocious news. Yet it didn't take too long until he was hooked. For a while, he'd gotten into the habit of putting off prayer and a peaceful conclusion to his day. Instead, he'd sit wide-eyed, staring at the screen, wondering what horrific event would be reported next.

That is, until one night when he'd watched and seen a photo of a young boy. The child had wandered from his home and had ultimately been brutally murdered. After that, Benjamin had never watched the news again. It made him feel too helpless. Too forlorn and powerless. Just as he felt now.

As they ran over the grassy area that joined their properties, he looked left to right and back again. Unfortunately, he couldn't spot any kind of tempting hideaway for an eight-year-old girl. And beyond the wide expanse of lawns, the only other things visible were tall, leafy hedges lining the rear of both their yards.

"Miriam, where on earth are you going?"

"Right over there."

She pointed to the middle of the row of shrubs. Yet he still couldn't make sense of where she was heading. It wasn't until they got closer, and he let his eyes roam above the hedges, that he saw massive outstretched branches pointing in every direction as well as up to the sky. It was then he remembered the ancient oak tree of his childhood. He also recalled the worn path between the set of shrubs that he'd taken numerous times so he could get to that magnificent work of *Gott*'s hands and climb it.

But little Emma? Would she do such a thing? His heart sank and his feet slowed, hardly believing that she would attempt climbing. Even so, as Miriam disappeared through the shrubs, he begrudgingly followed behind her. Until he heard Miriam let out a whimper. Then he took off running.

Leaf-covered offshoots flapped against his chest and pant legs until he came into the clearing that was home to the mighty hardwood tree. Immediately, he saw why Miriam had let out a cry. He nearly fell to his knees with relief.

On the other side of the tree, in a pinewood seated swing hanging from a limb nearly as round as a grown man's trunk, sat Emma. She didn't seem to notice their presence from where they stood. Or if she did, she didn't react to them. Instead, clutching her faceless doll to her chest, she appeared to be looking up into the clouds.

His heart twisted, overwhelmed with gratitude that she was safe. Yet also filled with deep sorrow for her loss.

"Is the swing new?" he asked Miriam.

"Somewhat. Your brother built it when Emma turned

five," she explained. "Roman made it so the three of them could enjoy it together. I know Lizzie had pictured Emma might be sitting there with her siblings one day," she said sadly. "When Roman asked if he could hang it from this tree, since it's mostly on our property, I was happy to oblige. On the rare occasions that I'd venture back here, it was a joy to see them sitting together. They looked so happy... so peaceful. I knew Emma would be here."

"What do I do?" he wondered out loud. "Do I scold her? Or warn her about the dangers of going off alone? Or—"

Miriam held up a hand. "You'll think of the right thing."

But as he dashed over to the swing, he found there was no thinking involved. He only did what he felt, what came naturally to him. He reached out and put his arms around his niece. He held her tight.

"Thank *Gott*, you're *oll recht*, Emma," he whispered. "Thank *Gott*, you're safe."

As he let loose his hold, he could see her *kapp* was on straight and not one of her blond hairs was out of place. There were no scratches on her freckled cheeks. The only disturbing thing he noticed was that, while thankful tears welled up in his eyes, Emma's stare was blank. If only she would say something. So badly, he wanted her to be able to verbalize every fear, hurt and disappointment in her heart. But, of course, she didn't speak. The only voice to be heard was Miriam's when she came up behind them.

"How about we go back to the house now? Don't iced tea and sugar cookies sound *gut*?"

Emma didn't smile at Miriam's suggestion. Even so, she obediently wriggled herself and her doll down from the swing. More than anything, he wanted to hold her hand all the way back to the house. Yet there was nothing that she needed protection from outside of a lingering aura of sadness. That dissipated slightly when they made their way into the house and kitchen. Emma sat down in her favorite chair while Miriam served iced tea and cookies.

Seeing his niece settled and safe, thankfulness welled up inside him in torrents. "I'm going to go put Joy back in the barn." His voice quaked as he grasped at any excuse to flee outside. "I'll run errands another day."

As soon as he was out the door, he bypassed the horse and headed for the nearest tree. Crossing his arms over the rough bark, he leaned his forehead against them. *"Danke, Gott! Danke!"* he said out loud, thanking the Lord for Emma's safety as tears ran down his cheeks.

He stayed that way for a while, silently praising *Gott* and wondering what was the next best step for his niece. When he heard footsteps come up behind him, he hurriedly swiped at his eyes. Turning, he faced Miriam.

"I saw Joy was still hitched and thought I'd check on you."

"You left Emma alone?"

"She's fine, Benjamin. She picked out a cookie and is taking her time with it. But you, on the other hand…you don't look so *gut*." Her brows drew together.

"I'm sure I don't," he admitted. "I've been doing some thinking, and I wish I wasn't saying this, but I think it might be best if Stephen and Angie take Emma. Plain and simple, I can cook and clean, and manage all kinds of things of my own and in a workplace. I've been doing that for years. But taking care of a child isn't like any of those things, ain't so? If you hadn't been here to help me find her—"

"Benjamin," she interrupted. "Don't be so hard on yourself. If *kinner* are good at anything, it's at keeping a person on their toes."

"But it's true, Miriam. I've been gone from here a long

time, and there are things I don't know about. She doesn't know me any better than she'd know Stephen and Angie. At least there'd be two of them to care for her." He glanced up into the cloudless sky, not wanting to say the next words out loud. "I'm going to write to my *bruder* and let him know to come get her when he's back in the States. I just have to figure out how to tell Emma." He let go of a long breath before looking into Miriam's eyes. "I hate to ask you, but since you know her better than me, can you help me do that?"

He knew it wouldn't be a comfortable conversation for either of them. But he didn't think it was an odd request, given that Miriam had earlier stated she thought making a home with Stephen and Angie was in Emma's best interest. Even so, she stood staring at him.

"*Nee*, Benjamin. *Nee*," she replied in that stony tone of hers. "I can't."

He tried to simply grit his teeth before unkind words spilled from his mouth. But, apparently, he didn't try hard enough. "Oh. Well, I am sorry that I asked. For sure I wouldn't want to burden you," he said caustically. "Why wouldn't you want to get back to doing the things that you do? Stay aloof. Keep distant. Not get involved."

After he spat out the words, he immediately regretted them. He was just about to apologize when a slight smile twitched at the corner of Miriam's mouth. That only heightened his frustration even more.

"You're smiling?"

She crossed her arms over her chest, peering at him. "You think you know me so well, don't you?"

"You're easy to know, Miriam. An open book as they say, Teacher."

"Would you listen to that? Benjamin Byler is talking to

me about books. Interesting…" she said, looking all around as if addressing an audience.

The slightest smile remained on her lips, but when her eyes landed back on his, he detected a shadow of hurt in them. And that made him feel awful.

"Look, Miriam," he went on. "I appreciate what you did today and what you've done so many days recently. But we should stop the bickering, don't you think? After everything that's happened today, I'm not in the mood. And, honestly, I have nothing else to say."

"Well, I do."

Of course, she did. Somehow, he managed to keep from rolling his eyes.

"Okay, then." He latched his hands onto his suspenders, trying to maintain his patience. "Say whatever it is you need to. Speak your mind."

"*Danke*. I'll do just that," she affirmed.

He prepared himself for a Miriam Schrock rant, but all was silent as he watched her creamy cheeks turn pink. Then rosy. And, finally, a deep crimson.

He became concerned. "Miriam, are you *oll recht*?"

She nodded. "*Jah*, why?"

"Well, because you said there was something you wanted to tell me, and you haven't spoken a word."

"Oh, that. I was just going to say…" She paused to clear her throat. "Even after the way you've been short with me just now, I'm ready to court you."

"You're what?" He shook his head in disbelief. "I don't understand. Earlier today, you said just the opposite."

"And a girl can change her mind, can't she? I *am* a girl, you know." Her hands flew to her hips. "Whether you think of me that way or not."

"But maybe it's not such a good idea. Like you said,

Stephen and Angie are two people who have a more stable life to offer Emma."

"But we're two people who can offer something that may be even better for her. At least, for right now anyway. And I wouldn't be saying that if I didn't believe it. Trust me, I want to court you about as much as you want to court me."

His head jerked at her frankness. Yet he didn't know why. Shouldn't he be getting used to her plainspokenness by now?

Only stopping to take a breath, she continued. "When I saw Emma sitting in the swing, I realized you're right, Benjamin. Though I hate to admit it. Emma shouldn't be shuttled off to some foreign place right now to be with people she doesn't know at all. If she's here, she can still be close to her *mamm* and *daed*'s memory. Whether that's being in the same house where they enjoyed life together. Or in the same yard. Or, like today, sitting in a swing that her father built while hugging the Amish doll her mother made. I'm sure all of that brought her *mamm* and *daed* nearer to her, remembering how it felt for the three of them to spend their time that way. I'm no doctor, but I think she needs those kinds of ties to Roman and Lizzie so she can heal."

That said, she looked at him. He knew she was waiting for a response, but he didn't know what to say. Seeming to realize that, she spoke up again.

"It's all up to you, Benjamin. I'm just saying, for Emma's sake, you can go ahead and ask me to court you again." She tilted her head. "That is, if you still want to."

Despite what had happened with Emma, she seemed to be so certain of what she was saying and what she was offering. He only wished he could be. But the gut-wrenching fear of what could've happened to his niece under his watch brought doubts creeping in. Question after question jumbled his mind. Was he honestly up to the task of figuring out what was right and healthy and safe for another human being on a day in, day out basis? Hadn't it taken him years to figure that out for himself?

Jah, he had heard what Miriam was saying. Even so, he stood still, staring while seeing nothing. He was too preoccupied, listening and hoping to hear an answer from his heart.

Chapter Three

Miriam held her breath as she stood facing Benjamin. Was he or wasn't he going to ask to court her a second time? Looking at him, she couldn't tell what was going on in his mind.

His brows were drawn together in such an agonizing expression, he hardly looked like the handsome catch that *maedels* proclaimed him to be. And his pensive, scrutinizing eyes kept staring at her, making her feel uncomfortable.

Finally, she turned her head, scratching the back of her neck simply to get out from under his gaze. All the while, she could only wonder self-consciously, was he rethinking Emma's situation? Or her as his partner?

Not that it would mean anything if he didn't ask again, she tried to convince herself. It wasn't like he'd be slighting her, right? They didn't have feelings for one another, after all.

Still...it will hurt even just a little if he doesn't ask. And you know it.

She tried to ignore that inner voice the best that she could. After all, the situation with Emma was far different, wasn't it? It wasn't like all those times in her life when she hadn't been invited somewhere. In Emma's case, she'd been invited, declined, then ultimately changed her mind.

But only because she wanted to honor Lizzie's and Roman's memories and do as much as she could for their sweet daughter.

And, even if she heard from Francie, she could deal with that later. She'd wait until things were more settled between Benjamin and Emma, and he had proven himself to Stephen. In the meantime, Emma would have happy, healing memories of the parents who were now gone from her life. That was so much more than Miriam had ever had.

Suddenly, she had to fight off the heaviness that wanted to settle in her heart. It was the same feeling that always caught her off guard when she recalled seeing her own father for the last time. Unfortunately, she could never, ever, forget how she'd watched her *daed* walk straight down their driveway one evening, autumn leaves swirling around his feet. Never once did he look back at what he was leaving behind. He simply disappeared into the grayness of dusk. For the longest time when each day dawned, she'd go to the window and watch for him, praying for his return. Those prayers were never answered.

Now, there was little she could say to Benjamin about Emma. For sure and certain, it was a hard decision he had to make. Even so, she didn't know how much longer she could withstand his silence. Her patience wearing thin, she spoke again.

"You look mighty lost in thought, Benjamin. But don't be stewing too long," she warned, holding her head high. "Some offers aren't *gut* forever, you know."

That said, she began to walk toward the house to check on Emma. Apparently, her movements drew Benjamin from his trance.

"Miriam!" he called.

She'd only gone two steps and turned to face him. *"Jah?"*

"There's something I want to say to you."

She cocked her head, crossing her arms over her chest as if only half interested, which was a pretense at best. Inwardly, she braced herself in case of Benjamin's rejection. "What might that be?"

"I want to tell you that Roman and I…" His voice instantly grew hoarse. "We, uh, see that hill over there?" He pointed to the farthest part of the Byler property where the level land took a hefty rise.

She glanced at the mound she'd seen plenty of times, striving to wrap her head around such an offhanded comment. "I see it, *jah*." She nodded.

"Well, when we were *youngies*," Benjamin continued, "Roman and I used to race on roller skates down that hill."

"That doesn't sound so smart."

"You're right. It's amazing we never got hurt, because we didn't just race. We had quite a time of it, playfully knocking into each other on our way down. Sometimes we'd even fall and be tumbling all over each other till we reached the bottom." He paused as if remembering. "I'd truly forgotten all about that when I first came back to town. Since the accident, though, every time I glance in that direction, I can see Roman and me there. And what's more, I remember exactly what it felt like to be with him."

He looked at the hill again before turning back to her. "To tell you the truth, my heart still aches, wishing he were here. But each time I glance at that hill, the pain is a little less. That's because I can hear his laughter ringing in my head. Lifting my heart. And the sound of it…" He paused. "It makes me smile." A sentimental grin tugged at the corner of his mouth. She thought she noticed moisture in his eyes. Hers were misting too.

"Miriam." He said her name in a kinder way than she

was used to. "I'm telling you this because it shows that what you're saying about memories is true. And when *Gott* first woke me up this morning, I had this idea about you and me in my head and how we could help Emma. I'm guessing time will tell if I'm the person who is supposed to be in her life. But until then, Miriam, I am asking again, do you—would you—want to walk out with me?"

At first, she thought her heart lightened because her offer hadn't been refused. Yet the joyful feeling that welled up inside her was so intense, she realized it had nothing to do with her. It was sheer hopefulness for the dear little girl she knew.

"*Jah*, I will walk out with you, Benjamin Byler," she stated as definitively as when teaching arithmetic in school.

"Like you said before, people aren't too likely to believe we're courting," he reminded her. "I'm sure they'll be talking about you and me."

"That will be nothing new in my world." Miriam smirked. "And, if it doesn't work out, at least we'll know that we tried. So, it's a deal then. We're courting for Emma."

"How do you want to get started?" Benjamin's blue eyes questioned hers.

"You're asking me?" She laughed. "Now that's funny, since you made my lack of experience in the courting department *verra, verra* clear and public when you first got back to town." How could she ever forget one of the more embarrassing evenings in her life? A night when she'd finally been invited to a party.

"I have no idea what you're talking about." He frowned.

"You don't, huh?" She shook her head, not sure if she believed the man she was about to walk out with or not. "Remember, the night of the gathering to welcome you home? All of your friends were there, and Lizzie, nice as she was, invited me to come too. You didn't notice me for the longest time. When you finally did, you drew all kinds of attention to me. You made a big announcement about how I should get an award for teaching longer than any woman in Sugarcreek's history."

"What's so wrong with that?" He shrugged. "I thought I was being nice."

"Well, I thought you were being snide, and I'm guessing everyone else must've thought the same because they all grew silent."

"*Jah*. I remember now. Why was that?"

"Seriously? You don't know? Most Amish women who are chosen to teach end up leaving after a couple of years. They go on to get married and have a house full of *kinner*."

"Oh. Well, I didn't mean to bring attention to your love life. And I still stand behind what I said. You should get a reward for teaching so many *kinner* year after year. You must be doing a *gut* job, and they're fortunate to have you."

She chuckled at the way he artfully rambled off a string of compliments. "Is this what you do with all the girls? Sweet talk them?"

"Is it working?" He lifted a brow, offering up a boyish grin.

"Not really." No way she was going to give him that kind of satisfaction and encouragement. "Now, about courting…" She changed the subject, aiming to keep their newly established relationship businesslike. "Do we start next week? Should we look at a calendar?"

"*Nee*. I think we should begin right away."

His answer caused an unexpected wave of dizziness. "Are you saying, like, now?" She pushed her eyeglasses up on her nose.

"*Jah*, we should start right this minute. Then I can write

to Stephen and let him know we're a couple. That may hold him off for a while."

She quivered as she realized she had no idea what was in store with this newfound, fabricated relationship.

"How, uh, how should we do that?" she stammered. "Start, I mean?"

"We could begin by taking Emma out to dinner this evening. Go to her favorite restaurant…" His forehead creased, as if trying to remember where that might be.

"Kauffman's Kitchen," she supplied, knowing how fond Emma was of their burgers and shakes. "I suppose we could," she agreed. "Better to jump right in before one of us gets cold feet."

She couldn't help but wonder what dress she would change into for dinner. Her favorite blue dress was dirty, and her plum-colored one needed ironing. Although she should have more than enough time to do that. Oh, but it wasn't as if she needed to look good for Benjamin, for sure and certain. Yet she did need to play the part of his date and play it well.

"I suppose we should go inside and tell Emma about our dinner plans then," she said.

"Let's do it." He nodded. "Ladies first."

Benjamin stretched out his arm, inviting her to go ahead of him.

Oh, how she could feel herself blush at his gesture. When was the last time anyone had done that for her?

"I know what I'm getting." Benjamin laid his menu aside. "Now, what do you two think Dolly would like to eat?"

He knew it was a silly thing to ask, but someone had to make conversation. Even if it was only in jest. Wasn't that the reason they were at Kauffman's Kitchen? For him and Miriam to appear to be enjoying each other's company in public?

He had to admit it was the strangest date he'd ever been on. A timid Emma sat across from him hugging her doll. Having a child along was a first for him since he'd started dating as a *youngie*. Also, ever since they'd arrived at the restaurant, Miriam had gone silent. She'd buried her head in the menu, seeming to study it as if preparing for an exam.

"Any ideas about Dolly's preferences, Miriam?" he prodded, trying to remain playful. What was going on with her anyway? She usually never stopped talking—or at least never quit giving her opinion. "Miriam?"

"Oh!" She lifted her head and set down the menu, placing one hand on top of the other on the table. "Let's see. I would think Dolly would want to share whatever Emma is having. And I'm guessing that would be a hamburger and French fries along with a chocolate shake. Am I right?" She turned to his niece.

A brief wave of brightness flickered in Emma's eyes. It was enough to make him feel like he'd been drenched in rays of sunshine.

"Well, *gut* to know." He smiled. "Because here comes our waitress now."

"Benjamin Byler!"

"Susan Raber. What a surprise!" The girl hadn't changed much in the years he'd been away. With such a pretty face and huge greenish-blue eyes, she was definitely memorable.

"I haven't seen you since you got back to town. It's *gut* to see you now, though. How are you doing?" She focused all her attention on him, completely ignoring Miriam and Emma.

"I'm doing *oll recht*," he said. "*Danke* for asking. How have you been?"

"I've been working a lot. But—" She shifted on her feet, eyeing him more closely. "I am off on Saturdays." She twirled a loose tendril of her reddish-blond hair around her finger before tucking it back under her *kapp*. It wasn't lost on him why she was sharing that information. But now that Emma and Miriam were in his life, the point was moot.

"It's *gut* they give you a break," he replied. "Everyone needs that, ain't so? That's why we came here together to enjoy dinner tonight, in fact."

Thinking that he needed to prove a point, he reached out and covered Miriam's hand with his own. He knew Susan couldn't see Miriam's hand tighten under his. He also hoped she hadn't heard Miriam's slight gasp. "Miriam, would you like to order for you and Emma?"

While he knew even a momentary display of affection wasn't the most proper Amish thing to do, it seemed to accomplish just what he'd hoped. Susan's mouth dropped open and stayed that way even after Miriam slowly pulled her hand out from under his.

"Aren't you sweet, Benjamin?" Miriam feigned a loving look his way before glancing up at Susan. "Emma and I will both have the same thing. Burgers, fries, and chocolate shakes."

"Make that three," he chimed in, hoping to make things easy for their waitress. Especially since she appeared too shocked to even pull her pad and pencil from her apron pocket.

He also gathered up their menus and tried to hand them to Susan. But a few moments elapsed before she appeared to come to her senses and take them from his hands. Then she couldn't seem to get away from their booth fast enough. That made him feel bad. Yet, when he stole a glance across the restaurant, he saw her whispering to the other waitresses, who looked their way. Proper or not, sore feelings or not, his plan had worked.

"Well, we said we'd be stirring up talk," Miriam said, obviously seeing what he was. "By the way, didn't you step out with Susan a few times when we were *verra* young?" she asked. Emma's eyes probed him too.

"You kept track of my dates?" That seemed more frightening than flattering.

"Ha. Hardly. Susan was one of my sister's friends. That's how I remember."

"How is Rebecca?" He hadn't seen her drop by Miriam's house and was glad to change the subject.

"Happy. I'm invited to her house for my nephew's first birthday tomorrow. I'm sure you and Emma could come along. There'll be plenty of cake." As she looked at Emma, he noticed the hopeful glint in her eyes. "Would you like to go?"

More than any female he'd ever encountered in his life, he found himself constantly hanging on young Emma's every movement and expression. When she didn't respond right away, his stomach churned, disappointment squelching his appetite. But then she looked up at Miriam and gave an approving nod. He suddenly felt like his appetite was back on track. And that was good because soon a different waitress was delivering their food to the table.

After bowing their heads in prayer, he picked up the oversize burger in his hands. "Everything looks mighty tasty. I hope Dolly likes it."

"Do you want to put Dolly in the seat between us, Emma?" Miriam asked.

Emma settled her doll on the cushion and then began eating. When Miriam snuck a glance at him and smiled, he knew exactly what she was thinking. He hadn't seen Emma embrace anything so much in a long while.

"It was a *gut* idea to come here, Benjamin. Don't you think so, Emma?" Miriam asked as she squirted a few dabs of ketchup onto her plate.

Again, his niece's eyebrows rose, but no words came. She simply continued to munch on her fries, which was a good enough answer for him.

"Plus, none of us has to cook tonight," Miriam continued. "Although you do like cooking, don't you?" She looked over at him.

He knew she was referring to his hopes of opening a wings-and-rings eatery, but he was glad she didn't go into details. Assuming Emma had overheard conversations between him and her *daed* about their restaurant plans, he was afraid it would stir up more sad memories.

"That depends on who I'm cooking for." He winked at Emma, which was probably a little too much too soon. She immediately lowered her head shyly.

Seeing her fries were disappearing quickly, he was about to offer her some of his when a hand came up from behind, clasping his shoulder. Looking up, he saw the owners of the Village Market come alongside him.

"Mr. and Mrs. Yoder, it's *gut* to see you."

"How are you doing, Benjamin?" A middle-aged man with a paunch, Levi Yoder's expression was filled with concern. "I know *Gott* has tested your faith much recently."

"I just keep trying to stay close to Him for comfort and direction," he answered honestly.

"Miriam." Levi's wife, Betty, looked to the other side of the booth. "I've heard from your *mamm* you've been helping Benjamin with babysitting."

"*Jah.* It's been my pleasure. Emma is the best." Miriam gazed at his niece.

He could feel his heart begin to beat rapidly. Should he

speak up or keep quiet? He wasn't sure. Until he looked across the table at Emma and had his answer.

"Miriam is more than a babysitter." He glanced up at the Yoders. "At least, she's become so much more than that to me…"

"Oh, do you mean…you two are…" Mrs. Yoder wagged a questioning finger between them.

Even Emma's forehead furrowed as she glanced back and forth at them.

He shrugged. "Beauty comes from ashes, they say."

To which Miriam sighed wistfully as she smiled.

"Isn't that interesting. *Verra* interesting…" Mrs. Yoder shook her head, openly stunned by the news. "Well, you two—I mean you all—enjoy your meal."

Even as she and her husband walked away, Benjamin knew the woman was surprised. Out of the corner of his eye, he noticed her turn back a few times with a curious gaze.

Meanwhile, he and Miriam ate all their dinner and got a carryout box for the leftovers of Emma's hamburger. By the time they left the restaurant, the air had cooled down to a pleasant temperature, which his horse, Joy, didn't appear to mind.

After settling Emma into the back of the buggy, with Dolly in her lap and an oversize multicolored lollipop in her hand, she didn't look happy exactly. But his niece didn't look pained either. He was thankful for that.

As Miriam sat beside him and they took off down the main street of town, his mind kept coming back to the word Mrs. Yoder had used. In a matter of hours, things had gotten interesting.

"What an evening, huh?" He glanced over at his pretend sweetheart.

"Jah." Miriam nodded, her eyes smiling his way. "Be-

tween Susan and Mrs. Yoder, I'd say the gossip mill will be churning out lots of talk about us. You aren't wasting any time, that's for sure. I almost fainted when you reached out and touched my hand!"

He'd been surprised himself. Not only by his own boldness, but oddly, Miriam's skin had been softer than he ever would've thought.

"It was you who said earlier that we needed to jump in. So, I followed your advice." He quirked a brow. "Even though you seemed mighty hesitant at first."

"Well, I'm sure you're used to dating, but I'm not. I was nervous that's all."

"You, nervous? Now that's hard to believe." He chuckled, considering her strong personality. "But you came around, especially when talking to the Yoders and batting your eyelashes at me. How'd you come up with that?"

"Oh, I'm a quick study." She waved a hand. "I looked at other couples at their tables and copied what I saw. But the best part of the evening was—"

"*Jah*, I know what you're going to say."

They glanced around at Emma seated behind them in the buggy. She was focused on her doll and didn't see them looking at her.

"She ate more than she has for weeks," he said softly.

"*Jah*, exactly. That was *wunderbaar*!"

They rode the rest of the way in contented silence. Once he pulled the buggy into his driveway, Miriam insisted on walking home alone. As she said out of Emma's hearing range, he needn't feel obligated to escort her since it hadn't been a real date.

An hour or so later, it was Emma's bedtime. Once again, he dreaded the nighttime regimen as much as she seemed to. Even though a soft breeze fluttered in her bedroom window and Dolly rested on her pillow, as always, Emma seemed stiff and uneasy lying in her own bed. He was sure it was a time of day that brought up many memories. Sadly, neither a good-night prayer nor anything he did or said could replace her *mamm* and *daed* putting her to bed.

"*Gut nacht,* sweet Emma," he said before leaving her room, not expecting a reply from her.

As always, he kept her door cracked open slightly. For peace of mind, he wanted to be able to peek in on her. But when he did, like so many nights, there was nothing soothing about what he saw. Like the anxious puppy his family had rescued when he was a young boy, his niece often had a hard time settling down to sleep. She'd start to doze off then jerk awake. One eye would open and then the other, as if doing her utmost to stay on guard. Her eyes would then drift closed once more. Then the process would begin all over again.

Lying in his own bed later that night, he hoped and prayed there'd come a time when Emma would fall asleep peacefully—and stay that way. For sure that would help him sleep easier too.

Chapter Four

❧

"Are you *oll recht*, Miriam? You seem nervous."

Benjamin's calming blue eyes as he gripped his horse's reins were diverted from the road long enough to look her way and should've helped to soothe Miriam. But it only unsettled her even more, realizing she hadn't been able to hide her unease. Even so, despite all the anxiety mounting inside her that always accompanied a visit with family, she pretended to be clueless about his observation.

"Why would you say that?"

"Because all your fingernails might be bitten down to the quick by the time that we get to your nephew's birthday celebration." Casting a glance at her hands, a thoughtful smile curved his lips. "Fortunately for you, your sister's house is around the next bend."

She self-consciously rubbed her palms together before pushing her eyeglasses up on her nose.

"And that's the other thing," Benjamin added. "You also readjust your glasses when you're uncomfortable."

He'd noticed that about her too? She hadn't even realized that about herself. It left her to wonder what else her shockingly observant neighbor might've taken note of. Feeling awkward, she smoothed her skirt then tucked her hands beneath the folds of her lilac-colored dress.

"It's easy to see you're worried about something. Are you afraid your sister may already know about…?" His left eyebrow rose a fraction.

"Us?" She filled in the obvious blank.

He nodded.

"Nee, nee," she replied confidently even though her forehead bunched together. "How could she? We only just went out in public for the first time last evening."

"Then are you concerned about bringing us along today?" He glanced over his shoulder at Emma, who was in the back of the buggy. Miriam took a peek too. With Dolly sitting next to her, Emma appeared comfortable, swaying in sync to Joy's relaxing clip-clop rhythm.

"Not a bit. When it comes to that, Rebecca is like you."

"I'm like your *schweschder*?" He snorted. "How is that?"

"You both are quite social." Unlike her, which she didn't bother to add since that was a well-known fact around town. When barely a teen, she'd purposefully become standoffish and curt. It was her way of keeping people at arm's length. After all, if her parents had hurt her, what would stop others from doing the same? Any invitations for singings, parties or game playing didn't come pouring in for her. Just for Rebecca, who enjoyed everyone's company, and everyone enjoyed hers.

"Also, Benjamin," she continued, "just to let you know, I called Rebecca from the phone shack last night and left a message about you both coming to the party. I'm sure there'll be plenty of food for lunch since my sister only knows how to cook two things, both being casseroles." She found herself rambling. "She'll either be serving an egg noodle and beef casserole or a cheesy hamburger casserole. Or both. Even my *mamm* has learned how to cook in these years she's been living in Rebecca and Jeremiah's *dawdi haus*. She moved there when they got married a few years ago."

Her mother's move hadn't surprised Miriam. Why would her mother stay in their family home with her when she could be with the daughter that she liked best?

"You say your *mamm* is just now learning?" He sounded incredulous. She was sure it must be surprising to someone who'd been a restaurant cook and had thoughts of opening his own eatery. Even when she'd go to his house to watch Emma, she'd catch a scent of something delicious he'd prepared.

"I should say she's relearning," Miriam corrected herself. "She did some cooking when Rebecca and I were *verra* young *kinner*."

"Then who cooked after that?"

She didn't want to sound boastful or resentful, so she was quiet. But her silence must've been enough of an answer for him.

"You did?" he asked.

"We had to eat, ain't so?" she replied matter-of-factly.

His eyes narrowed and she couldn't quite figure out what he was thinking. Then, nodding noncommittedly, he turned his full gaze back to the winding roadway. She was grateful he didn't press the issue. As much as she appreciated his kind interest, when it came to her family, where would she even begin?

With her mother, whom she felt had abandoned her, too, when she was nine? The mother whom she never felt particularly close to, especially after her *mamm* spent nearly a year lying in bed mourning her husband's departure, leaving everything inside and outside the house for Miriam to manage? Or how even after her *mamm* did find a job and went out to work, nothing much changed. Her mother always came home too tired to take care of her and Rebecca, once again leaving things for Miriam to handle.

Beyond that, in some ways she struggled with her relationship with her sister as well. How was it that sometimes she could be so jealous of her beautiful sibling and the life she had and yet, at the same time, still feel compelled to be a responsible big sister as she'd always had to be? Seeing Rebecca and her husband, Jeremiah, together, those conflicting feelings never ceased. Unfortunately, today was no different, she thought as their house came into view.

"Here we are now," she said, recognizing the dullness in her voice.

As she pointed up ahead, she also noticed that her nails did look a frightful mess. Oh, well. She'd never be the perfect-looking woman her charming sister was.

That was even more obvious when Benjamin pulled into Rebecca and Jeremiah's driveway. Benjamin had barely hitched Joy to a post, and she and Emma had hardly climbed down from the buggy, when Rebecca threw open the front door of her home.

"*Wilkumme, wilkumme.* It's *verra gut* to see you all!"

Her sister's smile dazzled like the noonday sun, and her sweetly gushing voice could have competed with any song sparrow in the vicinity. Miriam was completely unaccustomed to such a greeting. Typically, nothing but scented lavender plants and tall Shasta daisies lining the walkway to her sister's celestial blue door welcomed her. If it happened to be summer, that was.

But as she held on to the plastic holder containing the birthday cake that she and Emma had made for her nephew, she knew without a doubt that Rebecca's outgoing show of hospitality had nothing to do with her. Her sister's warmth was solely directed at Benjamin and Emma walking ahead of her.

Friendly as always, Benjamin responded right away. "*Danke* for having us."

Miriam was sure he was sincere. All morning, his face had held a smile as he'd traipsed in and out of the kitchen, waiting for her and Emma to be finished baking and ready to go. He seemed beside himself, so pleased to be able to take Emma to another outing that she might enjoy.

"Such a pretty day for little Aaron's party, Rebecca." Miriam spoke up, attempting to sound pleasant.

"Ain't so?" Her sister gave a brief glimpse into the sun-lit sky and the auburn highlights in her deep brown hair shone even more. Then, with a friendly swoop of her arms, she ushered them all into her lovely home.

As Miriam entered the large house, her mind went where it always did, wondering if Rebecca and Jeremiah would manage to fill all the bedrooms with *kinner* one day. She chided herself for thinking about things that didn't concern her. But it wasn't that easy to stop. Especially when Jeremiah immediately crossed the room with their one-year-old son nestled in his arms, looking delighted to be greeting everyone. While he and Rebecca and Benjamin were catching up, Emma appeared to be fascinated with baby Aaron, who reached down to tug on her *kapp*.

Meanwhile, Miriam noticed her mother coming from the kitchen. Whereas her sister's hello had been effusive, her *mamm*'s was bland.

"Why don't I take that into the kitchen?" She nodded to the cake holder in Miriam's grasp.

"I can do it, *Mamm*."

"Of course you can," her *mamm* agreed. Even so, her mother grabbed the cake and led the way, behaving like the head of the household. It seemed now that her mother was older and living in Rebecca and Jeremiah's *dawdi haus*, she had taken on that role wholeheartedly.

Maybe that just meant her mother had done some growing of her own, Miriam thought as she followed her into the kitchen. As her *mamm* directed her to set the cake holder on the counter, she reminded herself not to be so judgmental. Not like her mother, who removed the lid and cocked a brow.

"It looks *verra* sweet," her *mamm* commented.

"Cakes usually are." She struggled not to roll her eyes.

"I want to see!" Rebecca came breezing into the kitchen, all smiles. "Oh, Miriam, what a great job you did," she exclaimed. "How did you make the number one so well?"

"Believe me, it wasn't hard at all. Emma and I enjoyed coming up with different shades of blue frosting to ice the cake."

"I only wish it would stay this way forever. But you know our little *buwe* is going to smash it with his hands. I'll just say I'm sorry before he does."

"Rebecca, that's what the cake is for." Miriam grinned. "And you made a cake for the adults, didn't you, *Mamm*?" She turned to her mother.

Light entered her mother's eyes, looking proud of herself since she'd only started baking again in the past couple of years. But that gleam quickly faded.

"I did. But this morning I changed my mind about the frosting I wanted to use, and I ran to the Village Market."

Miriam instantly froze. Her cheeks flamed like they'd suddenly been lit on fire. She tried telling herself that a trip to Village Market didn't mean her mother had heard anything about her and Benjamin. But her inner voice wasn't too convincing.

"They do have the best icing there. Almost like home-made," Miriam said offhandedly as she picked up a slice of cucumber from a relish tray on the counter. Plopping it in her mouth, she wished she could cool her cheeks with it instead.

"Miriam, is there anything new going on with you?" Her mother's hands poised on her apron's waistband.

Heart racing, she worked to speak calmly. "I'm out of the school for the summer and have extra time available, if that's what you mean."

"To help babysit Emma?"

Miriam crooked a shoulder. "*Jah*, and I've been making strawberry jam too," she said. "Next time, I'll bring some for you." Not that she was looking forward to another visit any time soon.

Her mother exhaled so heavily that Miriam knew it to be a huge sigh of relief. Even Rebecca appeared to notice, looking confused as she glanced between them.

"Well, that's *gut* to know because I heard the most ridiculous gossip from Betty Yoder today." Her mother clucked. "And I hope for your sake she doesn't go spreading it around. Of course, I insisted it wasn't true since it could cause you plenty of embarrassment, Miriam. Something you don't need for sure!"

"Mrs. Yoder is always gossiping about something," Rebecca chimed in. "What did she say?"

Her *mamm* smiled slightly before answering. "Oh, she has some crazy notion that your sister and Benjamin are more than just friends."

Miriam could feel the burning in her cheeks spread down the length of her neck. "You think that would be crazy?"

"Oh, *jah*!" Her mother started to laugh. Rebecca chuckled more demurely, politely covering her mouth with her hand.

Insides seething, Miriam couldn't resist prodding. "You don't believe Benjamin and I are a match. Is that it?"

"You and the Byler boy?" Her *mamm* shook her head. "*Nee*, not at all."

"And why is that, *Mamm*? Because Benjamin is so good-looking? Or maybe just so likable?"

"Well, he's…he's…" Her mother faltered. "And you're…" she added inconclusively.

Even though her mother didn't utter one complete sentence, Miriam could only assume the varying inflections in her voice implied only positive attributes where Benjamin was concerned. But for her? Not so much.

Of course, it had never been lost on Miriam that Benjamin could easily fit into any circumstance or group of people and be accepted wholeheartedly. Just glancing into the other room, she watched him interact with Jeremiah's sister Amanda, his brother-in-law Clyde, and widowed father, Marvin, along with other guests who were arriving. She marveled at how powerful he looked, his chest broad, his shoulders square and solid. Yet no one was ever intimidated by him. Rather, everyone seemed to be happy around him. Whereas, generally, they avoided her. That was partially her own fault, true, since she'd made a habit of steering clear of others.

But her own mother thinking so poorly of her? The fact only deepened the hurt that never seemed to go away. She placed her arms across her chest as if that could suppress the intense ache in her heart.

"I suppose you'll just have to think it's *verrickt*, then, *Mamm*. Because it's so. As Mrs. Yoder said, Benjamin and I are far more than friends. We're officially courting."

Her mother gasped and Rebecca's eyes flashed wide, appearing more curious than criticizing.

"How could you, Miriam?" Her mother looked horrified. "I'm telling you, you're going to get hurt. And I'm only saying so to protect you."

Was her mother serious? When had she ever protected her from anything? Or taken on that kind of motherly role with her?

"Oh, right." Miriam couldn't help but scoff. "You mean you don't want me to court Benjamin, the popular guy in town because if our relationship doesn't work, it could mean a lot of gossip for our family. Is that what you're really getting at?"

Her *mamm's* cheeks reddened slightly at that.

"What I'm saying, Miriam, is that Benjamin knows more about the world than you do. You need to find someone less sophisticated. Someone more like…" Her mother glanced at the guests in the other room before setting her eyes back on Miriam. "Someone like Jeremiah, who makes your *schweschder* so *verra* happy."

After delivering both her warning and suggestion, her mother scurried from the kitchen. Miriam stood wide-eyed, stunned. If her *mamm* had stabbed her in the chest with a kitchen knife, it might not have hurt as much as her words had. For so many years when they were younger, Jeremiah, who was her own age, had visited their home frequently. They talked, played games with her sister, shared cupcakes she'd bake. He was the only person she ever trusted and let herself get close to. The only *buwe* she'd ever cared about. She was so sure they shared more than a friendship. And then one day it came to light that his visits had been all about love. But it wasn't love for her. Rather, he was in love with Rebecca. She couldn't fault her sister for being the woman of Jeremiah's heart. But the situation caused her to feel awkward around them for sure. It also caused her to shut herself off to love and others even more.

Fortunately, she was in no way expecting a long-term relationship with Benjamin. Even so, her mother's implications were clear. Obviously, from all that had been said and left unsaid, in her *mamm*'s eyes, Benjamin was a great catch but too much for her. And because of that, he was a man Miriam would never be able to hold on to. All of which stung even more.

"Miriam…" Rebecca immediately came to her side. "I'm so sorry," she said softly, consolingly. "*Mamm* is… you know… *Mamm*."

Placing her hand over Miriam's, Rebecca gave a gentle squeeze. And though everything inside her felt bitter and cold, for a moment her sister's touch didn't. It was a kind of warmth she hadn't felt in years.

Miriam had been right about what her sister would serve for lunch, Benjamin noted. He and all the other guests had enjoyed Rebecca's two types of casseroles, plus green beans, homemade biscuits, fresh fruit and veggies from relish trays. But then with full bellies all around, it was time for the main event—presenting Aaron with the birthday cake that Miriam and Emma had made. Standing in the Lapps' kitchen with Emma at his side, Benjamin realized he had plenty to smile about.

First, there was the sight of Rebecca and Jeremiah's entertaining one-year-old as he sat in his highchair, cooing delightedly. But that was only in between little Aaron digging his tiny fingernails into his very own yellow cake and then pulling out handfuls covered with every shade of blue icing. Some of which even ended up in his mouth, while most was spread all over his chubby face.

Then there was the sight of Emma. It was no contest which vision heartened him more. Though Emma hadn't ventured far from his or Miriam's side during the gathering, overall, she'd seemed to enjoy herself the entire time. Especially now. She stood grinning openly, and her eyes sparkled as she watched Aaron make a mess of himself along with his high chair and the floor. The keen joy Benjamin felt seeing her happily smiling and enjoying herself touched him deeply. And in a way he'd never experienced before. It felt like something he wanted to share.

Glancing in Miriam's direction, he hoped to get her attention. He wanted her to see what he saw in Emma. He wanted her to feel pleased by it too. But while everyone in the room was chuckling and caught up in the celebration, Miriam looked distant. Like she wasn't even there. It wasn't until it came time for Rebecca to open Aaron's gifts in the living room, that he saw Miriam crook a smile. That was when Rebecca handed over the wiped clean, little baby for Miriam to hold. But after the presents were opened and she deposited Aaron back into his *mamm*'s arms, her smile faded. And while the adults enjoyed slices of her *mamm*'s cake, she shuffled away to wash dishes.

An hour later, on the ride back home after the party, she seemed just as withdrawn, hardly saying a word. Although she did manage to put on a happier face for Emma's sake when she helped put his niece to bed.

But afterward, she appeared to want to leave quickly, heading for his front door.

"I'm going to get home now." She sighed. "It's been a long day."

"Too long to sit on the porch for a bit?" he asked. "The air has cooled down. I wouldn't mind some company."

In years past, he would've never guessed that a one-year-old's birthday celebration could wind up being a nice day for him. But it had been, and he wasn't ready for the day to end. He also hoped he might be able to help Miriam feel better, because it was obvious something was bothering her.

He offered up his most imploring look.

"I suppose I could," she acquiesced. "But only for a short while."

Although he hadn't been back in town that long before his brother and sister-in-law had passed, he'd picked up on many of their habits right away. As soon as he and Miriam stepped onto the porch, she settled into the Adirondack glider that he knew had always been Lizzie's favorite. He chose the deck chair most used by his brother.

Staring out into the yard, though the sky was darkening and night was falling, other creatures besides him were holding on to the day too. Lightning bugs blinked randomly as they floated in the air. Unseen crickets chirped constantly as if hoping to be heard. Even the distant hoots of a persistent owl traveled over the evening air.

Meanwhile, the two of them were silent until he finally spoke.

"*Danke* for inviting us today, Miriam. I could tell how much Emma enjoyed watching your nephew tear into the cake. She even smiled a lot when Aaron crawled over to her and tried to pull himself up using her leg."

"I was glad to see that."

"Were you? I would've never known. Not from the glum way you looked all afternoon, which I was sorry to see. I hope you don't mind me asking, but did something happen while we were there?"

"*Mamm* and Rebecca know, Benjamin."

"Know?" He blinked.

"About us, Benjamin. *Us.* There you go again. Even

you can't say the word that puts you and me together." She huffed. "Apparently, my *mamm* thinks our courting is the most ridiculous thing ever."

"You told her?"

"*Nee, nee.* We've never been close like that. She was at the Village Market this morning. Betty Yoder told her."

"Ah…" He was beginning to understand. "Well, I'm sorry she doesn't think much of me."

"Oh, you're not the one she doesn't have much regard for." Even in the dim light, he could see her lower lip tremble slightly. "But I shouldn't be griping at you. You can't help being an all-around *wunderbaar* man, perfect in everyone's eyes."

"Me, perfect?" He had to chuckle. "Eh, I don't think *Gott* would agree with that, especially since there ain't a perfect man alive, least of all me. My own mother wouldn't be quick to say so, either, if she were still alive. Neither would the girl I dated in Cincinnati."

That got her attention.

"You met an Amish *maedel* down there?"

"*Nee.*"

She sat up even straighter. "Oh, it was an *Englisch* girl?"

"*Jah.* Megan and I worked together at Wyatt's Wings and Rings, and I tried everything I could to make her happy. I got a cell phone, driver's license and leased a car. And I truly cared for her. But, out of the blue, she dumped me, as the *Englisch* are fond of saying."

"She quit you?" Miriam beamed.

"That's the first time I've seen you smile all day. So, my broken heart is something for you to grin about, huh?" He pretended to be hurt. Yet he was anything but. It seemed silly, but he was happy to see her mood shift, even at his expense.

"It's just that no one around these parts would believe a girl broke up with you. But then…" A slight shadow instantly crossed her face. "I don't know, Benjamin…"

"Don't know about what?"

"I know we've said people may not believe us. But after dealing with my own *mamm* today, I'm really not sure this is going to work between us."

"Does that mean…?" His breath caught like a young schoolboy waiting to hear the worst. Yet it wasn't a heartbreak he was worried about. It was Emma's well-being. "Are you thinking you want to quit before more people find out about *us*?"

"Quit?" Her voice ramped up, clearly offended. "I'm not one to quit. I made a promise, and I aim to keep it as long as I can."

Relieved, he began to exhale deeply until she added, "But—"

His breath hitched. "But what?"

"We should get things more settled. We need to move more quickly."

"Why? Is there some place you need to get going to?" he remarked, teasingly.

She blinked, looking more startled by his question than amused. Immediately, she got back on topic. "Starting tomorrow you should get Emma in the routine of doing chores again."

"Already?" His shoulders slumped.

"There's been enough time. People think I'm hard on students, but I believe giving them responsibilities lets them know they can depend on themselves. Besides, Emma used to hang laundry with Lizzie and even help her with cooking. I really believe she'd like doing those chores again, working side by side with you."

"I suppose," he said hesitantly. "But then, after chores, can we do something fun with her?"

She rolled her eyes. "You're such a pushover."

"How about we take her to Beachy's farm and market? She can pet the animals, get fried pies."

"Fine, fine. But one day *verra* soon you need to do something else."

"Like what?" He couldn't imagine.

"You should stop in at the location you and Roman had chosen for your restaurant."

"I don't know, Miriam. What if I open the restaurant and every time Emma sees it, it's a sad memory of what her *daed* had hoped to do? She may not be ready for that."

"And you may not be either. But you need to go anyway. Go see what needs to be done and decide if you want to do it. Don't forget, your *bruder* Stephen mentioned you needed a sweetheart *and* a steady income."

"Roman and I both had money saved up for the project…"

"*Gut!* Because, no matter what, you're going to need it." Spoken curtly in Miriam Schrock fashion, she stood to go. Politely, he rose too.

As he stood on his porch watching her cross their yards to her house, he shook his head. Strangely, he was getting used to Miriam's directness. More than that, after being in a few relationships with both Amish and *Englisch* females who'd kept him guessing, he was even beginning to appreciate it.

Chapter Five

❧

"You're doing a *verra gut* job, Emma."

Miriam complimented the young girl as Emma stood on tiptoes at the other end of the clothesline and pinned another of her dresses over the rope. The morning sun beat down on them without the slightest breeze to ruffle the damp clothes. Emma appeared just as unflappable, hanging one garment after another, the child seemingly set on her work.

Or were Emma's thoughts actually elsewhere? Such as missing her *mamm* by her side at a time like this?

Or could Emma simply be wondering how she'd gotten stuck with her *onkel*'s large pile of laundry—because Miriam certainly was. For sure and certain, something had gotten lost in translation from her discussion with Benjamin the night before. That was apparent when he'd come knocking on her door early in the morning, saying Emma was awake and ready to do laundry with *her*.

Not that she minded spending time with Emma. There was nothing else she'd rather be doing. And at least, after praising Emma about a job well done, the girl turned to look at her. A hint of a humble smile graced her lips as she brushed a blonde wisp of hair from her forehead. But then, all too quickly, Emma went back to her basket of laundry, seeming more adult than childlike, causing Miriam's heart to sink.

Even so, Miriam took Emma's cue. Bending over the brimming basket by her feet, she pulled out a pair of Benjamin's long pants. As she shook the trousers in the air to straighten them, she couldn't shake off her concerns about Emma so easily. All she could think as she took clothespins from her apron pocket and hung Benjamin's clothing was how much Emma reminded her of herself at that age. A realization that tightened everything inside of her.

In her mind, no child should have to deal with life's realities as a youth. Yet she knew plenty of her students who'd had to do just that. Her heart had gone out to those *kinner*, too, and she'd often felt at a loss. The most she could offer was extra support in their schoolwork to prop them up and keep them going. But with Emma, things were different. Hopefully, she and Benjamin could pave the way to Emma becoming a healed and happy child again. Even though their relationship was unusual.

As she picked up a pair of men's socks and pinned them to the line, she was immediately reminded of the uncomfortable encounter with her mother the day before. How she'd wanted to stomp out of Rebecca and Jeremiah's house and walk all the way to Elizabethtown to Francie's! She'd felt that full of steam.

But then she had glanced at Emma. She'd witnessed the girl's sweet smile while enjoying baby Aaron's antics. And in that moment, all the bitterness knotting her chest unraveled in waves, drowning out thoughts of her mother. It was replaced by hope and, for just a bit, she had smiled too. That had made her decide that no matter the cost, or how embarrassing things got, she wasn't giving up. Emma was worth the price.

Even if that included doing Benjamin's mountain of laundry.

She smiled inwardly as she glanced over at Lizzie and Roman's daughter and began to hum a hymn of praise. *Gott* hadn't blessed her with a voice nearly as lovely as Lizzie's, but she hummed anyway. All while trying to trust that the Lord wouldn't disappoint her. That one day, hopefully soon, Emma would hum along with her too.

"How come I have more laundry on the clothesline than anyone?"

She and Emma both jumped at the sound of Benjamin's voice from behind them. Turning to look at him, she gasped and Emma's hand flew to her mouth. Not only were his shirt and pants completely covered in thick mud, but he was caked with dirt from the tips of his fingers to his elbows. Muck also streaked his forehead and cheeks, concealing his good looks, which wasn't such a bad thing. Locks of his hair were clumped together with brown goo. Yet the man was grinning openly. Thankfully, for him, it didn't appear he'd ingested any sludge. His teeth still appeared clean and white.

"I think the answer is mighty easy to guess from the sight of you," Miriam quipped. "Wouldn't you say so, Emma?" She glanced at the girl who was now biting back a smile. "Is your *Onkel* Benjamin possibly the messiest person you've ever seen?"

Emma nodded, and Benjamin glanced down at his chest. He wiped at his shirt, which only covered it with more dirt instead of brushing away any grime.

"What happened to you?" Miriam asked.

"I was cleaning out the gutters from spring storms and I fell off the ladder into a muddy pit."

"Are you *oll recht*? Are you hurt?" Right away, she noticed Emma's small face contort with worry. Making her wish she hadn't asked.

"Not a bit," Benjamin answered readily. "The fall may have even knocked some sense into me. Enough that I came up with a *gut* idea." He glanced solely at Emma. "What if I get cleaned up and you and Miriam head over to Beachy's farm with me? I haven't petted any kid goats or lambs in a while. Would you like that?"

Emma's face lit up. Instantly, so did Benjamin's. Miriam had noticed lately that he watched Emma so carefully, so guardedly, that his expressions were often a reflection of his niece's. It made her wonder how she'd ever been so naïve to think that any person's existence was void of pain or hardship—even Benjamin's. Yes, he'd always seemed to have a blessed life, with everything good and easy, and going his way. But recently, he'd lost so much. She could tell by everything he did and said, he was afraid he might lose Emma too.

"If you *maedels* will let me help," he added with a glimmer in his eyes, "for sure and certain we can get the job done quicker."

He stepped closer and Miriam knew he was simply attempting to get a rise out of her and Emma. She was happy to play along.

"No way!" she yelped. "You're a filthy mess! Stand back!" She held up a restraining hand.

Keeping up his act, he made a slight lunge toward the container of freshly washed clothes. She deftly beat him to it, hugging the holder protectively. "Emma, hurry!" she shouted. "Guard your basket!"

Emma took the same shielding stance over her clean laundry. With that, Benjamin crossed one dirty arm over the other and frowned, pretending he was put off. "Really? You don't want my help?"

"*Nee!* Now, go," Miriam demanded, freeing up a hand

and pointing toward the house. "Go get yourself cleaned up. As dirty as you are, it's going to take forever. Beachy's may be closed before we get there."

"Then I won't take time to wash my hair."

Emma's eyes went wide at that. Miriam worked hard to keep from laughing and to keep her voice stern. "Oh, *jah,* you will, Benjamin Byler. Otherwise, Emma and I are leaving without you."

As he headed to the house, she looked over at Emma and shook her head. Smiling, she rolled her eyes. Emma followed suit and did the same, even seeming on the verge of a giggle.

Or am I only wishing for it?

Regardless, Miriam's heart was thumping happily as they both returned to their remaining laundry. Plucking the next item of clothing from her basket—Benjamin's white shirt—she found herself remembering how, just a few days ago, he'd shown up at her front door wearing it. She recalled, too, how the color of the glorious red and coral roses appeared more prominent as he'd held them against the white fabric covering his full chest. The white had also made his eyes gleam a brighter blue. Holding the shirt in her left hand, she took her time smoothing out the fabric with her right one. Somehow, she wanted to remove all the wrinkles for him.

And then she wondered why.

As Benjamin pulled into Beachy's parking lot with Emma and Miriam, he immediately began to have second thoughts. That was because the last time he'd been at the Amish farm and market, he'd been with... What was her name? He squinted, thinking. Tessa. Tessa Hochstetler. At sixteen, he'd just started his *rumspringa* and thought

Beachy's petting zoo would be a great place to bring a girl like Tessa. That way she'd see what a sensitive, caring guy he was. That had totally backfired within the first five minutes there. A llama had spit on Tessa, leaving a stain on her rose-colored dress. He'd never heard from her again.

However, when Emma eagerly hopped down from their parked buggy, that memory and his present concern dissipated quickly. He let out a pent-up breath, feeling thankful as he watched her. Looking as confident as he'd ever seen her, his niece strode in front of him and Miriam right up to the ticket booth at the entrance of the petting area. Only then did she glance back at him and Miriam. She eyed them down her nose, as if they were a pair of sluggish slowpokes.

Her enthusiasm brought a smile to his lips. Miriam chuckled under her breath.

"Good call coming here, Benjamin," she praised him.

Catching up with their young leader, he paid for their tickets as well as purchased three containers of sliced carrots to feed the animals. Taking the carrot holder in her hand, Emma rushed ahead of them once again, making her way into the oversize barn.

"Really good call," Miriam repeated as they followed behind her.

"Is that a compliment I'm hearing from you—and for the second time?"

"*Nee*, more of a statement of fact," she replied in prim Miriam fashion, though her dark blue eyes seemed to twinkle behind her glasses.

As Miriam got caught up feeding carrots to a pen full of piglets, he trailed behind Emma. Although he'd known his niece to be cuddly with her doll, seeing what a natural nurturer she was with the animals still took him by surprise. And warmed him too.

Without a lick of hesitation, the child approached every creature—lambs, piglets, goats, rabbits, llamas—and offered them slices of carrot. It was clear, though, that the kid goats were her favorite. The small creatures were as cute as puppies and seemed just as sweet. So was Emma's grin when a male kid sporting patches of black and white fur continued to stay close, reluctant to leave her side.

Finally, at the end of the rows of pens, Emma stopped and turned over her carrot holder to show the little guy it was empty. Undaunted, the kid stood on hind legs, leaning his front paws against the length of her dress.

"Emma, I have a few left." Benjamin offered her his last pieces of carrot. Then he stepped back to observe what looked to be a mutual attraction and attachment between his niece and the goat. Even once those slices were consumed, the pygmy goat still stayed where he was. With Emma gently stroking his back, her affection seemed to be just as palatable to the kid as an edible treat.

"His name is Bumper." Miriam came up beside him, a whiff of her lavender-scented shampoo arriving with her.

"How do you know?"

"There's a tag on his collar."

"I hadn't even noticed."

"I probably wouldn't have, either, but Clara Kilmer told me about him."

"Who's Clara Kilmer?"

"She works here. She's over by the piglets, in the light green dress."

He glanced over his shoulder to see who she was talking about.

"She's the mother of one of my students," Miriam informed him. Then, speaking in a lower voice, she added, "She also mentioned a couple of other interesting things."

"Jah?"

Miriam nodded. "Oh, yes. She said she's happy to hear that we're courting, since I've been alone and on my own year after year after…well, she had a long list of years."

"How did she even know?"

"From Aaron's party."

"But she wasn't there."

"I know. It seems after we left the party, Rebecca told her remaining guests about you and me courting. That included Jeremiah's older sister who is friends with Frieda Klinger, who's a neighbor of Clara's." She paused to take a breath. "Clara also gushed about how she's so *verra* glad we found each other."

He cocked a brow and chuckled. "Someone is *happy* for us? That's different."

"And nothing I would trust." Miriam waved a hand. "Knowing Clara the way I do, I hardly believe she's saying that out of kindness. Her son, Daniel, isn't one of my better students. But then, he rarely tries. I have to wonder if Clara's spewing compliments, hoping I'll give him better grades."

"But you'd never do that, would you?"

Miriam pulled back and looked him in the eye. "Thank you, Benjamin. Thank you for knowing that about me and realizing that I can't be bribed. Although…come to think of it, I was easily taken in by my *verra* caring neighbor." She started to smile then immediately blinked as if realizing how that may have sounded. "Er, I mean not taken in. More like I was pressured…coerced… Oh, whatever the word is."

Her cheeks instantly flushed, and knowing she felt awkward because he did, too, he tried to make light of things.

"I think you could say we formed a partnership. Hey,

would you look at that?" He nodded toward Emma. "The two of them look like a *gut* partnership too."

"Well…" Miriam took on her business-as-usual tone. "Clara also noticed Bumper's fondness for Emma and mentioned that the kid is for sale."

"What?" A rush of joy jolted him. "You mean we could take him home?"

"I'm just delivering the message."

"But something new for Emma to love?" The thought came forth unbidden from his mouth.

"And more responsibility and another mouth to feed, Benjamin."

"A *verra* small mouth, Miriam," he countered.

"Even so, you do know that cute, playfully mischievous kids can grow up to be destructive old goats, don't you?" True to her nature, Miriam had to remind him of every negative. He would've been shocked if she hadn't. Only, this time, he was feeling too good to let her spoil his mood.

"*Jah*, but it's the same with all species. Even humans, ain't so?"

Her lips curved slightly. "You have a point."

"Emma." He instantly directed his attention to his niece before Miriam could add more of her two cents' worth. "What would you think about taking this kid named Bumper home?"

All at once, Emma's coloring heightened. Her cheeks blushed and her eyes sparkled. She nodded eagerly, wrapping her arms around the furry creature.

"However," he said as sternly as he could, "you'll be Bumper's main caretaker. I can teach you how to feed him, brush him, and so on, but he'll be your responsibility."

Her face split into a wide grin and she buried her head in Bumper's fur. Obviously, she hadn't said a word, but he took that as a yes.

Despite Miriam's initial comments, he thought he noted sentimental specks of moisture in her eyes as they both stood watching Emma. "You're a *gut onkel*, Benjamin," she said.

"What? Another compliment from you today?" He jested.

"Just another statement of fact." She smiled.

Between Miriam's verbal pat on the back and Emma's noticeable happiness, he was feeling mighty good as he waved Clara over. While Clara led him and Bumper to the cashier at the front of the building, Miriam and Emma crossed over to Beachy's market, eager to shop for fried pies and a new leash just Bumper's size.

"Bumper is a sweet kid," the cashier told him after ringing up the purchase and giving Benjamin a receipt. "And *Gott* made him to be sensitive, too, from what we've seen."

"How so?"

"Well, one morning we came to work and found a pony hitched to the railing over there." She pointed to the stalls on the other side of the lot. "Someone left it there, probably because the poor creature was *verra* despondent. They get that way sometimes, you know, when they lose another horse who's been a companion to them." She gave him a knowing look. "Anyway, when we took the pony in, it wasn't too long before Bumper started paying the pony visits. Let me tell you, that little pygmy goat was like one of those therapy dogs you hear about." The lady nodded to Bumper. "Soon, the pony rallied and got comfortable and even happy in its new surroundings."

After hearing that, Benjamin was even more pleased they'd made the trip to Beachy's. As he walked away and stood outside the market, waiting for Miriam and Emma, he held Bumper in his arms, close to his chest. Stroking the kid near its furry little ear, Bumper snuggled closer, seeming content. Bumper wasn't the only one being soothed.

"Little guy, I have a feeling you're not only going to be *gut* for Emma, but for the rest of us too."

He rubbed his cheek against Bumper's and could've reveled in the relaxing moment for a while longer. But that wasn't meant to be. A group of boisterous teenaged *Englisch* boys came around the corner of the building from the ice cream truck parked there. In rumpled baseball uniforms, they looked sweaty but victorious. Each one carried a double scoop ice cream cone in his hand like a triumphant trophy for a game well played. He started to smile, calling to mind his own baseball wins back in the day. Until he saw *him.* Spotted *him* in the crowd.

All at once, Benjamin's breath hitched. His body stiffened every which way, intensifying his grip on Bumper. While he jaw clenched, his heart pounded as if drumsticks were beating against his chest.

There he was. Ethan Caldwell.

The boy who'd killed Roman and Lizzie.

Benjamin hadn't laid eyes on the teen since the day of the accident. Never once encountered him in their small town. Yet he'd always imagined, when that time came, he'd be as forgiving as he had been during the entire tragic event. After all, Roy Caldwell's son hadn't meant to run into Roman and Lizzie's buggy. Ethan hadn't meant to harm anyone. The boy hadn't set out on a mission to leave Emma an orphan for the rest of her life.

No, as a newly licensed driver, Ethan had only been trying to avoid hitting a deer in the road. Simple as that. And that's when he'd lost control of his car. Running headlong into Roman and Lizzie, the buggy flipped over, hurling down a hill.

Everything about the incident spelled accident, completely and totally. That's why Benjamin had never pressed charges against him. He hadn't wanted someone so young to suffer too.

So why, then was he feeling so angry? Why was everything roiling inside him? Was it because Ethan was going on with his life like nothing had happened? While everything had changed in Benjamin's life and Emma's?

"Benjamin, you'll never guess who I saw."

Miriam's voice startled him. Her remark did also. He spun around to look at her and Emma, their arms laden with shopping bags.

Had Miriam seen Ethan and recognized him? But no, she couldn't have. The noisy team of boys had already passed by. Everything around him was quiet again. All except for Miriam.

"We saw Hannah Burkholder. She invited Emma to come over and play with Sarah any time that—" Miriam stopped. Her brows pulled together, eyeing him uncertainly. "Benjamin, what's wrong?"

"Nothing, I'm fine."

"You don't look fine," she pressed.

She could already read him that well?

"Miriam," he uttered her name tersely. "I said, all is *gut*," he fibbed, working to loosen every taut muscle in his body. "I'm ready to get home so Emma can feed Bumper, and I can eat a fried pie."

Miriam seemed mildly satisfied with that response, not questioning him again as they crossed over the parking lot to the reserved hitching area. After Emma boarded the buggy, he lifted Bumper into the back seat with her. Meanwhile, Miriam took her usual spot next to him up front, shopping bags creating extra distance between them.

And he felt distant. Anytime he glanced at Miriam or Emma throughout the ride, they both looked happy as could be. Bumper appeared comfortable as well. He only wished he could feel the same. But how could he? His insides were knotted in torment.

Had he only pretended to forgive Ethan to look like a devout Amish believer in everyone's eyes? Was he that hypocritical? If he had truly forgiven the teen, would he have reacted the way he had? Was he holding on to resentment, incapable of truly forgiving? That's not what his brother and sister-in-law would want from him. And not what *Gott* expected of him.

As Joy meandered along, barely needing his assistance, he glanced up at the sky. Being a person who was unable to forgive wasn't the way he wanted to live his life either.

Chapter Six

Ever since the trip to Beachy's the week before, Miriam couldn't help thinking about the signs of distress she'd seen shadow Benjamin's face right before they'd left that day. She didn't know if she'd caught him off guard, thinking of Lizzie and Roman. If so, she could relate. From time to time, she'd catch herself having moments like that too.

Or had he been worried about keeping them all safe on the buggy ride back home? Or maybe having second thoughts about her? Bumper? Even Emma?

For sure and certain, something had been on his mind that he'd refused to share. Not that it was any of her business, but it did make her curious. Thankfully, she hadn't noticed any hints of that stressfulness lately. That was particularly true this morning as she made the short walk over to his front yard. Even though he was having a hard time coaxing Emma to cease her galloping around the field with the baby goat, the straw hat shielding his features from the sun couldn't hide the satisfied expression on his face. No doubt, he'd been right. The child was delighting in something new to love.

"You can play chase with Bumper one last time, Emma. Then we really need to get going," Benjamin called out to her. "Miriam is waiting for us."

"Actually, I'm right here." She sauntered up to his side, smiling at the sight of the playful pair.

"Hey." He dipped his head. "I thought we were supposed to pick you up."

"Not to worry. I made the trek across our lawns safely." She grinned. "Has Emma been out there since dawn romping with her new best friend?"

"Oh, *jah*. Just like every day since we brought that spotted kid home."

"I'd offer to stay here with her if Hannah wasn't expecting her to come play with Sarah this morning."

"*Nee, danke.* I think it's good she's going to the Burkholders'. She needs to play with a real friend, not a furry one, for a change," he said. Miriam couldn't have agreed more. "Maybe playing with Sarah will help her to…" He paused. "You know…"

Turning his eyes back to the field, he sighed and didn't have to say more. She knew exactly what he was talking about and bit her lip before words poured out of her, telling him how she'd been thinking the same thing for days. How each day since she'd run into Hannah at Beachy's, she'd been looking forward to this scheduled play date for Emma. That she'd been praying Emma would be so engrossed in enjoying time spent with Sarah that she'd blurt out something. Anything. Even one little word.

"Besides…" Benjamin faced her again. "You were the one who said I need to start figuring out making a living. So, you're not getting out of coming to town with me and checking out the place Roman and I had in mind. I'd like your honest opinion on things."

Warmth flowed through her the same way it had the first time he'd mentioned making the trip to the restaurant site with him. To think a man—this good-looking man in particular—wanted her thoughts truly did make her feel appreciated in a way she wasn't accustomed to. Chuckling uneasily, she shooed away the foreign feeling best she could.

"You say that now," she quipped.

"You're right. I'll probably live to regret it." He pursed his lips seriously. Yet his eyes twinkled at her teasingly. Immediately, her cheeks heated. As much as she wanted to believe that warmth was from the summer sun, she knew better. Just his eyes resting on hers made her blush. And she'd been blushing too much lately. That wasn't good at all.

And why? It wasn't like he was her beau or anything.

Hoping that he didn't notice, she quirked a brow and peered over her glasses. With her most authoritative teacher tone, she jested right back. "Uh-uh. Can't have it both ways, Mr. Byler. Do you want my thoughts about your possible venture or not?"

"*Jah.* Sure. I value your opinion."

"Just don't forget you said that when the time comes."

"I'll try my hardest not to." Then he laughed, and another odd feeling came over her. She couldn't believe how much she enjoyed making him do that.

In the past weeks, they'd gone from squabbling with each other to playfully jibing one another. That wasn't a bad thing, especially where Emma was concerned. But it did make her feel closer to him than before. Given their relationship was pretend, that was unsettling.

"We do need to get on our way, don't we?" he asked.

"*Jah.* I'd say so. I told Hannah we'd be there around ten."

"Emma," he called to his niece again, "it's time for Bumper to go in his stall."

They both directed their attention to the reason for them standing there together. Emma. Eyeing her as she led Bumper to the barn, they watched some more as she exited the shelter and came walking slowly toward them.

"It's also *gut* that we'll be in town and people will see us together some more," Benjamin said.

"*Verra* true." Prior to her new partnership with Benjamin, Miriam never concerned herself much about what to wear. She'd simply throw on any old frock, as long as it was clean and free of wrinkles. And why not? No one noticed her anyway.

These days, however, being anywhere at all by Benjamin's side, she not only *felt* on display. She *was* on display. Knowing that, she'd donned her favorite sky-blue dress for the outing and brushed her thick black hair thoroughly before creating a tight bun and adding her *kapp*. In her sister's old bedroom closet, she even found a pair of Rebecca's slip-on sneakers. Nicer than her everyday sneakers, they were just as comfortable.

Of course, once the three of them were settled into the buggy and Joy's hooves sounded on the pavement, she looked over at Benjamin and doubted he'd labored one second over what to wear. Granted, most men probably didn't. And in his case, his casualness really didn't matter. His shirt could've been blue instead of a pale gray, his hair under his straw hat could've been neatly combed instead of messy. Her neighbor still would've been a treat for most women's eyes. Not that she considered herself to be in that group, given their situation.

Yet, once they'd dropped off Emma and headed down the winding road toward town, suddenly everything felt different. Usually, she'd be talking a mile a minute with Emma in the back seat. Not only did she do it to fill the silence but, deep down, she hoped it might be a way to get Emma to respond. But now there was no Emma. And that was the problem, wasn't it? Ever since their first day together, she and Benjamin had never been alone. Sure, Emma wasn't always right by their sides, but she'd been close by. The young girl had been akin to their chaperone, their distraction.

Without Emma, all at once, Miriam felt awkward in Benjamin's presence. Overly aware of him sitting by her side, her heartbeat quickened. Her mouth went dry. What had she gotten herself into?

"I have to say, it's mighty unnerving when you're quiet," Benjamin said, interrupting her thoughts.

She looked at him and frowned. Tried to find her voice. "I thought… I thought you'd like me that way for a change."

"I thought so too." The corner of his mouth curved slightly upward. "But, honestly, it's strange. I'm used to you speaking your mind. Continually. Are you worried about Emma? Should I be worried too?"

"*Nee*, Benjamin." She sat straighter. "You know Hannah and Jake. Or at least you used to. They can't be any nicer, and they've raised their *kinner* that way too. And I know Sarah is a *verra* sweet *maedel* since I've had her as a student." She paused. "Don't worry. Even if Emma doesn't talk, Hannah will make sure the children all treat her well."

His jaw muscles visibly relaxed as he loosened his grip on the reins and sat back on the seat. Miriam was glad he was taking her word for it, and she knew Lizzie would've said the same thing. Lizzie and Roman had been good friends with the Burkholders ever since their daughters had become pals.

"I, uh, I just thought of something…" Benjamin looked over at her. She noticed his hands tighten on the reins.

"*Jah?*"

"Usually it's not just the two of us. You and me. Usually we're with Emma," he said, surprisingly mirroring her thoughts.

"I know." She pushed up her glasses on her nose.

"From the look on your face, are you thinking that's a bad thing?"

"*Nee*. It's just… I…" she stammered, her brain scrambling for a way to defuse the subject.

"Don't you worry." He held up a free hand. "It'll only be a few hours that you have to put up with me. I hope you can stand me for that long."

With that last comment, she wasn't sure if he was poking fun or being serious. Maybe a little of both?

Given that they'd be alone together for hours yet, she preferred to keep matters light. Wiping her brow, she let go of a wearisome, exaggerated sigh. "I hope I can, too, Benjamin. Maybe a *gut* lunch later will make up for the time spent with you."

She expected him to chuckle or groan kiddingly. Instead, he replied, "I'd be *verra* happy to take you to lunch, Miriam. Very glad to."

He sounded beyond sincere, causing her mouth to feel full of cotton all over again. She'd only meant they'd eat once they got back home. No way did she expect an invitation to dine out.

Shaking her head, she made a point of looking away from him, setting her gaze on the rural landscape flowing past her side of the buggy. But it wasn't anything she saw that brought a slight smile to her face. No, it was the fact that she'd been glad she'd worn one of her best-looking dresses for their outing today.

As Benjamin approached the abandoned restaurant with Miriam, he noticed the windows were even dustier than when he'd last been there with Roman. Since hardly any sunlight shone through the glass, he turned on all the overhead lights when he ushered Miriam through the front door.

"The old Miller Pancake House? This is the place you and Roman were considering?" she asked. "I can't believe Lizzie never told me."

She appeared somewhat crushed, and he started to lay a comforting hand on her shoulder. But he held back, opting for an imploring look instead. "Please don't feel bad, Miriam. Roman and I asked Lizzie not to share the details with anyone. And, honestly, for a while we didn't know how things were going to turn out. So, there wasn't much to tell."

"How so?"

"Well, none of Isaac's offspring from around Sugarcreek wanted to take over the restaurant. They only wanted to keep the building and lease it. I think they'd grown up living the restaurant life and were tired of it. But a son of his who lives in Kentucky kept acting like he might rekindle the business. So, we put a bid in, letting them know we were interested, in case that didn't happen. And when it didn't, we signed a lease agreement. But then the accident happened, and I wasn't sure..." His voice drifted as a wave of melancholy came over him.

How many times did he have to remind himself that Roman and Lizzie were with *Gott*? Clearing his throat, he added, "Isaac's son, Henry, who has been handling things, has been incredibly patient with me and my indecision. But once again, you're right. He's been starting to pressure me lately, and rightfully so. The family needs an answer from me soon."

"It looks like there's plenty of work to do here." He watched her gaze up at the crack in the ceiling over her head. Paint had obviously been flaking off for some time, creating a pile on the floor. "You sure wouldn't want any of that to get into someone's meal."

"Ha! *Jah*, we mentioned that to Henry. It's caused by a leak in the roof."

"Ah...would those repairs be at your expense or theirs?"

"Funny you should ask. He never gave us a solid answer about that."

"I'd say it's their building, it's their responsibility. I wouldn't pay a cent for it."

Although she'd always had a reputation for speaking her mind, he was beginning to admire that in her. At least she was honest. A person always knew where you stood with her. "You have a matter-of-fact way about you."

She shrugged. "I don't believe it's something you need to be diplomatic about. Or..." Tapping her lip with her forefinger, he could tell she was conjuring up something. "Do you know how much the materials will cost to repair the roof and inside here?"

"I haven't checked on it yet."

"Well, if it's not too costly, maybe you can make them a deal. Tell Henry that you'll get it fixed, which I'm sure you and your handy friends can do easily. But in return, he'll need to give you a couple months free on your lease while you're getting your restaurant established."

"That's a thought."

He was about to add it was a mighty good idea. But she'd already moved on, swiping her hand across a dirty tabletop. "The place sure needs some cleaning up. Everything is so—ah...ah...ahchoo!"

"*Gott segen eich*. It's dusty in here, I know."

"Some of the vinyl cushions on the chairs are torn too. I guess a lot of people sat in them."

Her comment made him wonder if Miriam had ever eaten

at the pancake house before or after her father walked out on them. Whereas, he could recall coming to the restaurant plenty of times with his family. That was another reason he and Roman had liked the place.

"I wish I knew for sure if barbecued wings and onion rings will put diners in these chairs again. I mean not the torn chairs. They'll need replacing."

"I've never had the kind of food you're speaking of, but I do know people like barbecued ribs. And plenty of *Englisch* tourists visit our town. They're probably familiar with the food you'd be serving. Besides that, everyone in town likes you, Benjamin. I'm sure they'll be wanting to see you succeed. However—" She pointed a finger. "If you decide to do this, I'd start getting more Amish folks used to the food. Bring some wings and rings to Sunday worship or have *youngies* bring them to singings."

"You always have good ideas, you know that?"

He thought he saw her blushing at his comment, but it was hard to tell since she immediately headed over to the kitchen.

"You can still smell the bacon grease in here, ain't so?" She chuckled.

"*Jah*. No doubt about that."

"Do the appliances all work?" she asked, glancing around the area.

"They do. Roman and I checked them out. But some will need to be replaced to cook wings and rings. Fortunately, my former boss has been waiting to sell me his used deep-vat fryers at a mighty good cost."

"Is there anything else you need to buy?"

"There's a few other kitchen items. Roman and I had also set aside money to refinish the hardwood floors and paint the place. I'll need to purchase a sign. Then there's the roof issue."

She leaned against the stove, crossing her arms over her chest. "I don't get it, Benjamin."

"Get what?"

"You said you wanted me to come to give my opinion on things, but it seems to me that you and Roman had everything pretty much figured out."

Feeling caught, his jaw clenched. Mirroring her stance, he leaned against the refrigerator opposite her, crossing his arms over his chest. Taking in a deep breath, he let out an equally long sigh. "I, uh, I'm sorry, Miriam. I should've been more up-front with you."

Silently, she questioned him with her eyes.

"What I mean is…what the truth is… I needed you here with me. *Jah*, I wanted you to see the place. That's true. But mostly the thought of walking in here by myself without my *bruder*…" He shook his head. "I couldn't do it. I couldn't face it alone. When I went to get the key from Henry, you're the person that…" He wasn't sure how to explain himself. Yes, he knew plenty of people in town, like she was always saying. Even so, in the past few weeks, Miriam was the person he felt the closest to. The person he trusted the most. Imagine that! Quickly he was coming to realize why Lizzie and Roman were so close to her.

He quirked a brow, not sure what kind of response he'd get from her. When she stepped forward and gently touched his arm, a silent grateful prayer flew heavenward.

"There's nothing to be sorry about, Benjamin. Not for a minute. You've had a lot to test your heart and your faith lately. But here's what I'm thinking, in case you want to know."

In the past, he may have been hesitant to hear what

Miriam had to say, but here, lately, that wasn't so. "I do." He nodded.

"This seems like it's been a dream of yours for a while and, like the Amish say, 'No dream comes true unless you get up and get to work.' I'm guessing it's why you came back here?"

"*Jah.* And you know those two older brothers of mine. They wanted different kinds of lives, and it made me want the best of both. To be a businessman like Stephen and baptized Amish like Roman."

"Well, what I was going to say is, if you do decide to go ahead with the restaurant, I don't think you should view it as if you're working toward this dream alone. It's something Roman wanted too. And who knows? Maybe Emma will want to work here or take it over one day."

"But I keep wondering what Lizzie and Roman would think of me doing this. Would they think I'm not spending enough time with Emma?"

"Do you imagine you're the only one in the world who has to balance family and work?" she mildly scolded. "Plus, you're capable, and everyone likes you. If you ask for help, like you asked me, you'll get it from people around here, and from *Gott* too."

People really had Miriam all wrong. *He'd* had her all wrong. She was caring and kind and sensible.

"You're a wise woman, you know that?"

"Well, *jah!*" She looked at him as if he were a derelict. "I *am* a schoolteacher, ain't so?"

As she smiled, he found himself noticing how her blue eyes shone. Not only that, he couldn't stop from grinning back. Never would he have guessed what a fun side Miriam had to her.

"*Danke*, Miriam. *Danke* for coming with me. You've

helped me decide. I'm going to try to make Roman's dream come true—and mine too."

"*Gut.* I have every confidence in you, Benjamin."

"*Jah*? Even though I'm the one who came to you asking for help with schoolwork back in the day?"

"Well, you were smart enough to come to the right person, weren't you?"

He threw his head back and laughed in a deep, jovial way. Something that he hadn't done for months. And he didn't know if he was imagining it, but the sound seemed as if it broke through the air and filled the space, replacing the sadness that had hovered over him when they'd first walked in the door.

Overwhelmed with gratitude, he smiled at her and wanted to return the favor. But the most he could think to offer once again was lunch. "I promised to take you out to eat. Would you still like to go, I hope?"

"That would be *wunderbaar.*"

Together, they started for the door, but before they reached it, it opened and in came a pretty face they were both familiar with.

"Ben, I thought that was you. I saw you through the window. What are you doing here?"

"Actually, Rachel, we were just leaving," he told Bishop Gingerich's daughter, avoiding her question.

"Heading anywhere special?" she asked.

Glancing between the two women staring at him, he wasn't sure how to answer that. If he said no, Miriam might think he wasn't considering their lunch together to be much of anything. If he answered yes, knowing Rachel, she may ask to tag along.

"I guess we'll know when we get there," he replied vaguely.

Even though being in the middle of the two *maedels*

made him feel uncomfortable, that feeling quickly sub-
sided when he ushered them outside. Turning the lock on
the door of his soon-to-be restaurant, his heart felt lighter
and brighter than it had in a long time.

Chapter Seven

The Corner Café wasn't all that crowded when Miriam walked in with Benjamin. Even so, Miriam noticed there were a few lunchgoers who thankfully didn't acknowledge their entrance. Then some offered welcoming nods while another handful gave them surprised looks. The same kind of dubious, baffled glances that Rachel Gingerich had given them. Well, given to *her* mostly. Rachel had saved her more charming gazes for Benjamin.

After being seated and placing their order with the waitress, Esther Klein, a quiet *maedel* they'd grown up with, Miriam found herself still stewing about Rachel. If only the bishop's daughter had never wandered into the former pancake house. Especially since Miriam had been enjoying the time with Benjamin so much. She'd been deeply touched that he'd chosen her, of all people, to accompany him there. She'd been moved that such a man would let her see him so vulnerable. Even more, he seemed to think enough of her to comfortably bare his heart with her, disclose his fears, share his dream. And then in walked Rachel, looking down her nose at Miriam and—

"Maybe you should've asked Rachel to lunch instead of me," she blurted out and then immediately regretted it. What was it about Benjamin Byler? She could usually keep her feelings to herself, keep others at arm's length, and not let anyone know her thoughts. But around him? That wasn't always so. She sounded like a jealous schoolgirl. It needed to stop. But truly, given the choice, wouldn't any man rather be sitting across the table from Rachel with her soulful brown eyes instead of her?

"Rachel? Seriously?" He forehead creased. "Is that what this is about? Why you haven't said hardly a word since we left Miller's old place?"

"Nee," she replied, being far from truthful. "I just... I had nothing much to say."

"But now you do?" A smile twitched at his lips.

Obviously, he was onto her. Even so, his voice was sweet. Something she wasn't used to. Uncomfortable, she shifted in her seat and pushed her glasses higher on her nose. Realizing what she'd done and that he'd noticed it, too, she shook her head at him. "Go ahead. Say it."

"Say what? I didn't see a thing." He chuckled.

His grin widened and, suddenly, the all-too-familiar warmth sparked and began to heat her cheeks. "You don't have to keep looking at me," she said calmly, although her stomach was in knots, still completely embarrassed by her outburst. Glancing around the room, she hoped to get out from under the gaze of the best-looking man in the entire restaurant. And she doubted that was solely her opinion.

"Where am I supposed to look?"

His question drew her eyes back on him.

"I don't know. Around somewhere." Anywhere but at her.

"You *do* know that Rachel isn't my type of *maedel*, don't you?"

"Oh, *jah*." Now she couldn't help but look him straight

in the eye. "I'm sure you'd never want to be seen with the prettiest girl in our community."

"She is one of the prettier girls. But only one of them, Miriam. There are others. Like the *maedel* I'm sitting across from."

She wasn't sure how to react. His compliment was like nothing she'd heard from a man before. Even so, taken at face value, it was simply a flattering remark, wasn't it? While it may mean something to her, it meant nothing between them. They were merely neighbors turned friends, right?

"Benjamin, you don't have to say nice things like that. It's not like anyone is close enough to hear."

"I know I don't. But a fact is a fact."

"Really, there's no need to act all charming. It's wasted on me," she said as she felt her cheeks redden even more.

"Whew!" He whistled, wiping his brow as if relieved, making her laugh.

"Whew what?"

"Glad I haven't lost my charm."

Miriam laughed again. She truly enjoyed being in his company and was beginning to feel a certain ease with him, just like she'd had with Lizzie and Roman. Maybe the Byler family simply had a way of making others feel good.

"*Danke* for putting up with me, Benjamin." She sighed.

"I could say the same," he answered. "At least you're the kind of girl that what you see is what you get." He took a sip of water before continuing. "I know I shouldn't speak ill of anyone, but Rachel is not the kind of girl I'm eager to get close to."

That took her aback. Was he serious? With all hints of pleasure gone from his eyes, he certainly looked like he was. "Why is that?"

"She's a fisherwoman."

"I don't understand. You don't like *maedels* who fish?" She frowned.

"Not like her. Even when we were young, she was the kind of girl who was always stirring the waters. She's looking for a boy to catch. As soon as she finds someone to her liking, she reels him in. Then she's quick to toss him back in the water. Nothing feels genuine about her because it isn't. I don't know if you'd ever heard how my friend Jonah Hershberger was hurting for a long time after their relationship ended."

"Oh, I forgot about that." She hadn't been in their social group when they were *youngies*. But she'd overheard others at worship talking about Jonah's broken heart. "Then you didn't have to experience Rachel's fishing for yourself?"

"Nope, not since witnessing it firsthand. With Jonah, and Roman too."

"Some men may have been prideful enough to imagine they'd have a different outcome with her."

"That would be just plain stupid. And pride does come before a fall."

Benjamin Byler did keep surprising her. He was strong yet vulnerable, popular but not boastful, good-looking yet modest. She could have gone on, but Esther showed up at their table bearing plates.

"Here's your club sandwich, Miriam, and your BLT." She set them both down, hesitating to say Benjamin's name.

"*Danke*, Esther," Miriam said.

"*Jah, danke,*" Benjamin replied.

"You're *wilkumme*," Esther answered. "Is there anything else you need?"

"*Nee*. It looks *gut*," Miriam said.

Benjamin nodded as he picked up half of his sandwich.

Instead of leaving them alone to eat, Esther kept standing there, and began wringing her hands.

Miriam gave her a questioning look. "Are you *oll recht,* Esther?"

"I just want to say *danke* to you too." She nodded to Miriam. "To both of you." She gave Benjamin a noticeably shy glance, and Miriam understood why. As far as she knew, Esther shared Miriam's romantic history, meaning she lacked experience with men.

"Why thank us?" Miriam was completely confused.

"Well, my cousin Mary heard from Ruth Troyer about the two of you being a couple and—"

"Wait. Ruth Troyer?" Miriam interjected. Ruth was the mother of one of her students, and she hadn't run into her since school had been out. "How would Ruth know?" she asked.

"I think Anna Stoltz told her after Anna had heard it from Sadie Lehman. And if Sadie Lehman says something," Esther said definitively, "you know it's true. She's doesn't make up things."

Miriam's mind began reeling. She glanced at wide-eyed Benjamin, who hadn't taken a bite of his sandwich yet. Sadie's husband was a deacon, and Miriam knew her to be a solid person for sure and certain. Yet she was older than them, so it was a bit puzzling that she knew.

"How did Sadie find out?" she asked.

"Maybe from Betty Yoder? They are *gut* friends, and the Yoders know everyone." Esther waved a hand, ready to dismiss who said what to whom. She seemed to have something more on her mind. "Anyway, when Mary told my *mamm* and me about you two, we were thrilled."

"You were?" Miriam's brow crinkled.

Esther nodded vigorously. "Oh, *jah*! My cousin Mary was too. It's proof to us. Undeniable proof."

Again, Miriam looked over at Benjamin and was glad to see he appeared as bewildered as she was.

"Proof?" he asked.

"Absolutely!" Esther's voice shrilled. "With you two being together, why it proves that the unbelievable can happen. When it comes to love, I need to keep trusting *Gott*."

Benjamin was visibly caught off guard. Miriam felt the same as she watched his mouth drop open.

"*Gott* does do wondrous things," he replied.

"Truly." Esther crossed her hands over her heart. "Enjoy your lunch and one another, you two."

"We will enjoy the food, *danke*, Esther. And we do enjoy each other, don't we, Miriam?"

"Us?" Her voice cracked, causing her to cough. When she caught her breath, Esther was still staring at her, obviously awaiting her reply. "*Jah*, we do," she answered, speaking the truth. Her truth. Even so, Esther's announcement was like a stake in her heart. As she'd told Benjamin when their fake relationship first began, no one would ever think of the two of them as a likely couple. As much as she enjoyed his company, and his smile warmed her heart, she couldn't even conceive of the idea herself. Why wouldn't Esther and her *mamm* and cousin be thinking the same?

While Esther's comment came from a sweet place, it was an eye-opener, reminding her of the ultimate truth. Benjamin hadn't asked to court her for real. He'd made the plea for Emma's sake. That meant that, just as he was making plans for his future, she needed to do the same.

Fortunately, she'd written to Francie before their partnership had begun. But when would Francie's reply come? Most importantly, what would her cousin have to say?

* * *

By the time Benjamin left the café with Miriam, the sky was becoming overcast. For the last part of lunch, their time together had seemed to grow cloudy too. For whatever reason, as they ate their sandwiches and then waited for the check, Miriam appeared pensive and quiet—a sure sign something wasn't right with her. Or maybe it was him. Perhaps she had tired of him as quickly as he'd thought she might. They had spent a long morning together, after all. In his mind, it had been a very special morning.

Walking next to her to the spot where his horse was hitched, he felt glad once again that he'd followed his gut in asking her to come with him to Miller's former establishment. There hadn't been anyone else he could imagine making the trip with him. For some reason, he felt safe confiding in her. And who else but Miriam would be candid and not just say what she thought he'd want to hear? Miriam had prodded. She'd been encouraging yet realistic. She'd helped set him on course. Overall, she'd been there for him. For that, he'd be forever grateful.

Once he helped her into the buggy, then seated himself beside her and began to steer Joy down the street, he was about to thank her again for everything she'd done. But before he could, she spoke up.

"You don't have to help me into the buggy like you did, Benjamin."

Confused, he dipped his straw hat at her. "I know you're a capable, self-sufficient woman, Miriam. But isn't helping a *maedel* into a buggy the right thing to do?"

"But there was no one passing by to see us. So, you needn't have bothered."

"And you needn't get so upset with me, Miriam." Her voice had sounded touchy, and his didn't sound much better.

He paused, working to calm himself. "Look, I won't do it again if you don't want me to. It was just my way of showing respect and appreciation for you."

"Oh…" She bit her lip. "Sorry."

"Nothing to be sorry about." At first, he hesitated to say more. Then he couldn't stop himself. "Miriam, having you go with me to the restaurant space this morning was life-changing for me. You helped me more than you could ever imagine. I hope you know that. And I hope one day you'll look back and say to people, 'See that wings and rings place? It's there because of me.'"

She giggled. Finally! The sound was music to his ears. "I don't think anyone will believe that."

"Oh, yeah? Well, I will," he said, wishing he could truly convey all the appreciation he felt. "And when Emma grows up, she'll know the part you played too."

"*Jah*, well…we'll see…" She rolled her eyes, and he knew she was embarrassed by his compliment. Right away, she shifted the focus from them to Emma.

"I'm sure she had a *gut* time with Sarah today."

"You think so?" he asked.

She nodded decisively. "At school, they do really well with each other."

"That's good to know."

Though Miriam sounded positive, he could see her hands were clasped together tightly in her lap. No doubt she had the same thoughts he did about Emma. Had Emma gotten carried away playing and uttered a single word with her friend?

Silence fell over them both as Joy's hooves created a soothing rhythm on the road. Even so, Benjamin felt anything but relaxed on the way to the Burkholders'.

He tensed even more the moment Miriam hopped out

of the buggy and headed for the Burkholders' front door. After knocking lightly, a half minute later Hannah opened the door surrounded by her *kinner* and Emma.

"The girls had fun," he heard Hannah report to Miriam. "Didn't you, girls?"

He watched both girls look at one another and grin.

"I'm sure they did," Miriam replied. "Next time, you can come to Emma's house and play, Sarah. Would you like to do that?"

Sarah nodded as her smile widened.

"*Oll recht.* Well, we better get going so you all can get on with your day." Miriam placed her hands on top of Emma's shoulders.

"'Bye, Emma." Sarah's voice was clear and bright.

He held his breath, hoping to hear the same from his niece. Emma merely smiled and waved.

As she did, he watched Miriam look over the *kinner*'s heads at Hannah. He was sure Hannah was seeing a question in Miriam's eyes. The same question he had on his mind.

Immediately, his jaw tightened. Watching for Hannah's answer, he prayed she'd tell them that Emma had spoken out loud. But with a sorry expression, Hannah shook her head.

Immediately, his heart sank. He was sure Miriam's probably had too. But as soon as the girls got in the buggy, Miriam didn't skip a beat. She turned to look at Emma in the back seat and began chatting as if Emma's muteness was nothing out of the ordinary.

"I bet it was fun seeing Sarah, *jah*? And those twins." She whistled. "Clara and Eli are *verra* cute, but they sure have a twinkle in their eyes. I wonder if they'll be a handful when they start school one day."

Without taking a breath, she went on to talk about how much time was left in the summer before school started.

She suggested she and Emma make banana nut bread one day soon. Then she mentioned she'd bought some carrots for Bumper in case Emma ran out. In short, she talked on and on. He could barely get a word in edgewise. But couldn't have cared less. Because each time he turned to look at his niece, a sweet smile was etched on her face. As Joy pulled them down the road, somehow Miriam's caring voice and all her chatter had the same soothing effect on Emma as it was having on him.

He might have been disappointed earlier when he'd seen Hannah shake her head, but Emma's grin right now was all that mattered.

Once again, he realized, it was all because of Miriam.

He glanced over at the *maedel* he was "courting" these days and instantly felt guilty. Like others, he'd always thought of Miriam as a curt, standoffish person. But hadn't he been the ungenerous one, so quick to judge without taking the time to know her? For sure and certain, she was anything but uncaring and unsympathetic. He could now hear that in her voice and see it in her eyes. Eyes that were sparkling in the sunshine as she talked to Emma, surrounded by features far prettier than Rachel Gingerich's. If only Miriam herself believed that to be true.

Maybe what Esther Klein had said about divine intervention may not have been so outlandish. Weeks ago, hadn't it been a nudge from *Gott* that had sent him grudgingly walking over to Miriam's house with a bouquet of roses?

As it turned out, that had been the best thing for Emma so far. If he was being straight with himself, maybe it was best for him too.

Chapter Eight

"Would you like to stay for a while?"

It came as a surprise to Miriam that Benjamin posed the question as soon as they arrived back at his house from the Burkholders'.

She hesitated at first, wondering if he was only being polite. After all, hadn't he had enough of her for one day? Yet when she dared to look closely at his tan, handsome face, she saw his invitation came with a hopeful glint in his eyes. And maybe even a hint of dismay too. They'd both been praying that Emma would start talking again at Sarah's. It was disheartening that it hadn't happened. As a teacher, however, she had to keep reminding herself that, so many times, things didn't click with students until they suddenly did.

Even so, Emma was managing to communicate in her own way. Right after Benjamin pitched his question, the young girl turned to her with a pleading look in her shiny blue eyes. Miriam couldn't resist.

"*Jah*, I can stay."

Her heart swelled at noticing how pleased Benjamin and Emma both appeared to be about her sticking around with them. The feeling didn't stop even when Emma immediately went running toward the barn to let Bumper out of his stall.

"She may not be talking, but at least she seems to be happy." Miriam sighed.

"That has a lot to do with you, Miriam."

Self-conscious, she waved a hand. "I don't know about that. I'd say Bumper is in the lead."

"But you help us both. And I'd *verra* much like to do something nice for you," he said sincerely.

Her cheeks heated and, since the sky had become grayer, no doubt the warmth wasn't from the sun.

"You did, Benjamin. Remember? You took me to lunch. Besides," she hurried on, "there's nothing I need." She wasn't about to explain how being with him and Emma the past few weeks made the summer days seem not as long and lonely as they normally did.

"You can't think of anything?" he prodded.

She looked off into the meadow at a playful Emma and Bumper to avoid his kind gaze. "Sure," she said. "You can, uh, teach me about goats."

"Goats?" He blinked, appearing befuddled. "You sure you don't need anything fixed around your house instead?"

"Not that I can think of. And I should know more about goats so when it comes up in the classroom, I'll be more knowledgeable."

"Seriously? You never had one?"

"*Nee.* I had enough trouble just taking care of the humans in my house."

He laughed, but it was true. "All right then," he said. "Let's go."

"Go where?"

The words barely left her mouth when he unexpectedly grabbed her hand and ran toward Emma. What could she do but hold on tight and keep up?

By the time they got close to Emma, the child was taking a break from playing chase with Bumper. She was petting the kid instead.

"Emma, your teacher here wants to learn more about goats, especially this cute guy."

Emma replied with a smile.

"First thing I told Emma about is food." He looked at Miriam. "Because food is what keeps us all going, right? Along with each other." He winked at his niece.

"Now, Emma knows that Bumper needs to be fed two to three times a day," Benjamin told her. "That will keep him healthy and fit. But if you see him getting a little weight on him, Miriam, that may be because Emma likes to give him lots of treats too. Don't you, niece?" He smiled at the little girl, who returned his grin.

"Two to three times a day. Noted," Miriam said. "And, *jah*, when I went to make stew for you two, I did notice most of the carrots were gone. That's why I bought more. But I figured Emma can't help that she's a sweet, nurturing girl. Can you?"

Emma playfully shook her head.

"Oh, and I just thought of something," Benjamin said. "Emma, this is something I forgot to show you." He bent down on one knee in front of Bumper and lifted the kid's foot. Holding it loosely, he turned it so they could see the underside.

"See how Bumper's hoof is curved?"

She and Emma nodded.

"Sometimes something will get stuck in there and Bumper may start limping. But even if that doesn't happen, you should still check the area regularly and make sure there's no grass or stones or—"

Suddenly, Bumper tugged his foot out from Benjamin's grasp. In the same motion, the creature clamped his mouth around Benjamin's straw hat, pulling it off his head. He reached out, trying to grab it, but Bumper was too quick for him. The kid took off running in a flash.

"Hey, my hat!" Benjamin yelped.

He jumped to his feet and looked like he was about to chase after Bumper, but then a sound erupted into the air, stopping him cold. It was laughter. A peal of laughter coming from Emma. A sound none of them had heard for what felt like forever.

Right away, Emma's hand flew to her mouth. Eyes wide, she seemed as shocked as they were. But then, so visibly tickled by the funny incident, there was no stopping the joyful noise that kept bubbling out of her. Her giggling even trailed behind her as she dashed over the field toward Bumper.

Miriam had had incidents with students who'd finally overcome or mastered a problem, and there was satisfaction in that and happiness for the child. That was for sure. But this? It was all overwhelming. She wasn't usually a crier. Yet tears of the happiest kind began streaming down her cheeks.

"Oh, Benjamin!" She turned to him.

His eyes were full of moisture too. His voice was hoarse when he spoke. "She's laughing, Miriam, laughing!"

"Praise *Gott*!" she uttered.

Without a moment's hesitation, he pulled her into his arms and hugged her tight. Exuberant, she clung to him as if they'd reached the peak of a mountaintop together. Overjoyed, she let him lift her into the air. Yet as soon as her feet touched the earth again, her senses seemed to take hold too. As they broke apart and stared at each other, Benjamin appeared taken back. She wasn't sure how to read his expression. Had he felt anything more than pure jubilation with her in his embrace? She was afraid to think that she had.

Feeling awkward, she tucked a wisp of hair into her *kapp*. Looking confounded, he ruffled a hand through his brown hair.

"You need your hat," she suggested.

"You're right. I do."

He almost looked as relieved as she felt that she'd distracted them both. Even so, her heart was skipping faster than her feet as they made their way across the grass to Emma. Benjamin was first to reach the spot where Emma was giggling as she tried to pull her uncle's hat from Bumper's mouth. With his niece's permission, Benjamin stepped in and wrangled the hat away, placing it on his head.

Emma pointed at him, laughing even more. The ripped hat did look comical, the brim hanging almost down to his nose. Miriam couldn't resist pulling the torn-up thing from his head and tossing it back to Bumper.

"Three against one," she teased Benjamin.

With that, she grabbed Emma's hand and, with Bumper alongside them, they romped ahead of Benjamin. He chased after them and probably could've easily caught them, but that wouldn't have been as much fun.

As they ran their hearts out, the dreary-looking clouds finally broke open. The rain started drizzling at first, but the droplets couldn't dampen their moods. Even when the rainfall became an official summer shower, all four of them continued circling the meadow.

In her entire life, she'd watched her neighbors play in the rain. Sometimes running errands in town as a teen, she'd see *youngies* having fun, skipping through puddles during a shower. But she'd never gotten the chance to do such a playful, childish thing. Not when as a young girl her life had been all about managing a house and the people in it.

She stopped for a minute to catch her breath. Wet locks of hair had fallen out from her *kapp*, landing on her shoulders. Her favorite dress was completely drenched, and Rebecca's stylish sneakers were covered in mud. Even so, all at once, an unfamiliar sort of pleasure welled up in her as she watched the man she was "courting" and the child she was so fond of, enjoying time in the rain. She didn't know what tomorrow would hold for her. But right now, her heart was overflowing.

Oh, dear Gott, *I'm soaked!* she giggled. *Soaked in happiness!* Danke!

Hours later, when the rain finally ended, Benjamin escorted Emma to Miriam's house for dinner. Seated around Miriam's kitchen table, he could tell he and Miriam were of the same mind and heart when it came to Emma. All throughout the meal, they both talked to each other and Emma as they always had. Neither of them acted as if it were a big deal that Emma had begun to talk some. Also, neither of them pressed her to say more than what she was comfortable with, which wasn't much.

Even though Emma's issue was both delicate and weighty, the way he and Miriam were handling the situation reminded him of a more frivolous incident when he was around Emma's age. Back then, he'd refused to eat peanut butter and jelly sandwiches for three weeks because Stephen had teased him repeatedly about not being manly enough to eat bologna. Wanting to impress his oldest brother, he switched up his lunch fare, pinching his nose while he ate the bologna sandwich. After a while, though, he tired of it all. He got up the nerve to tell Stephen to back off and pushed the bologna away. He returned to eating his favorite kind of sandwich. What he recalled most during those weeks was how his *mamm* had never nagged him to eat anything. She'd acted like she hadn't noticed. She'd let nature take its course.

Thankfully, time and *Gott* seemed to be doing the same for Emma.

"That was the best dinner I've ever had," he exclaimed, setting his empty plate aside.

Miriam rolled her eyes at him. "Your *onkel* likes to exaggerate, doesn't he?" She turned to Emma, who gave her a questioning look. "What I mean is, he likes to make a big deal of things."

A smile twitched at Emma's lips. *"Jah."*

Even the sound of one syllable coming from his niece's mouth left him grinning. "I'm not exaggerating."

"I'd say you are," Miriam countered. "I overcooked the chicken and the sweet potato casserole wasn't *verra* sweet."

"It all tasted *gut* to me. I appreciate you inviting us. I'm sure Emma does too." He glanced at this niece. "She's probably tired of my cooking."

"At least my dessert turned out better than the meal. I can promise you that."

"I can't wait!" he said sincerely, rubbing his hands together.

Miriam jumped up from her chair and began to clear their plates from the table. He started to help, but she insisted he stay put.

"This will only take a minute," she claimed. True to her word, dessert plates and clean utensils quickly replaced the dirty dishes.

Next, she set down a pie dish then a gallon of vanilla

ice cream. He wasn't a dessert expert, but the latticed crust looked familiar to him.

"Is that apple pie?" he asked. Picking up his fork, he leaned in closer to inspect it. Miriam waved a paring knife, gently shooing his hand away.

"*Jah*, it is. And still a bit warm. I hope you like it." She began slicing.

"I'm sure I'll love it," he replied.

"*Mamm* liked apple best," Emma said softly.

Miriam's knife halted in midair. His heart stopped as well. Looking at him, Miriam closed her eyes and shook her head as if to say she was sorry. He took that to mean she'd known that about Lizzie but had forgotten. He shrugged, a part of him thinking maybe it was a good thing after all. It was the first time Emma had spoken of her parents since the accident. Still, he held his breath and didn't doubt for a second that Miriam was holding hers.

Would Emma's comment be followed with tears? Would she clam up once again?

Finally, their answer came.

"I like apple best too," Emma said.

He let out an audible sigh. Miriam swiped her free hand across her forehead. "I'm glad," she told his niece and switched to a pie server. "Here's a big piece for you."

His niece started to pick up her fork then stopped to face him.

"Is there pie in Heaven?" she asked.

Seeing the concern etching every feature of her face was heartbreaking to him. Instantly, he felt heavy with sadness that this sweet child would have to ask such a question. Placing a hand over hers, he tried to answer the best he could, in a way that was both comforting and truthful.

"Don't you worry, Emma." He squeezed her hand. "I'm

sure *Gott* gives your *mamm* and *daed* every *wunderbaar* thing that there is in Heaven. After all, He gave them the most wonderful *gut* thing on earth—you!"

Her little face broke into a smile. She wasn't the only one. Miriam's lips curved upward as she nodded her approval to him. Then Miriam got back to business, holding an abundantly large scoop of ice cream over Emma's plate.

"Is this too much for you?" Miriam asked his niece.

Shaking her head no, Emma's eyes grew wide.

"Do I get that much too?" he quipped, acting silly for his niece's benefit.

Pretending to be exasperated, Miriam put a hand to her hip. "Not if you keep interrupting me, you won't."

"I'll help wash dishes if you give me a lot," he offered.

"Oh, *oll recht*." She then plopped an equally large scoop on his plate.

During dessert and dishwashing, Emma didn't say much more. In fact, after a while, he noticed that it was mostly yawns that escaped her mouth. Her eyelids began to droop as well.

As ribbons of pinks and oranges streaked the sunset, he and Emma thanked Miriam for her hospitality and then headed home. After all that had taken place during the day, it was obvious Emma was worn out. He didn't even need to coax her to get ready for bedtime.

Once she slipped into bed, he began their nightly routine. After saying a prayer over her, he gently squeezed her hand.

"*Gut nacht,* sweet Emma," he said in a hushed voice.

"*Gut nacht, Onkel,*" she answered softly.

Hearing those words, he nearly gasped into the silence of the room. How many nights had he listened and longed to end their day together that way? But even more special was watching Emma. On this night, she didn't need the security of Dolly cuddled in her arms. She didn't stare up at the ceiling like she had so often, too uneasy to close her eyes. Rather, she turned over on her side and snuggled into her mattress and pillow, her arm curled under her head. At last, she really did look peaceful and settled in for sweet dreams.

Leaving the door slightly ajar as usual, he walked down the hallway into the front room. As he gazed out the window, the sky had darkened, preparing most every creature for sleep. Yet everything inside him felt awake, stirred with happiness. In his heart, he praised *Gott* again and again for Emma's breakthrough that day. In his mind, he wanted nothing more than to have Miriam right alongside him so he could share what had just happened with the person he felt closest to.

Looking over at her house next door, he realized that growing up, he'd rarely taken the time to notice it there. It could've been miles away. Now it didn't—*she* didn't—feel close enough.

He shook his head in wonder. Of all people, Miriam Schrock! Who would've ever imagined such a thing?

Chapter Nine

Several days later, Miriam led a happy Emma into Sugarcreek's only shoe store to pick out a new pair of sneakers for her growing feet. Although it wasn't unusual for the child to frolic barefoot outside, Benjamin didn't want Emma anywhere near the rundown restaurant without her feet being covered. He feared she might step on something dangerous, like nails. When he'd asked if Miriam would take Emma for shoes, she had gladly agreed. A little shopping and then a visit to the former pancake house sounded like a good day for them both.

Yet as she held Emma's hand and guided her toward the children's section of the store, a now-familiar feeling washed over her once again. Too many times when she was with Emma or with the child and Benjamin eating, playing, walking or cleaning, she experienced a close attachment like she'd never known. Sometimes the feeling felt so natural, she didn't think about it. Other times, while it warmed her heart, it disturbed her, too, so afraid of where their time together may or may not be leading to.

But right now, she wasn't at the Shoe Rack to dwell on herself or the future.

"Emma, your last pair of shoes were a size two, I believe. So, you may be ready for a size three. Do you see any here?"

She'd already spied where the threes were located, but she let Emma scan the rows.

"Here's some." Pointing to the right, Emma walked toward them.

"*Gut* find." Miriam stepped near her. "Do you see any style you like best? Any that you'd like to try on?"

Emma's head swiveled back and forth. "These?" She shyly picked up a pair of white sneakers that had a narrow band of light pink on the sides.

"Sure." Miriam nodded. "They look nice."

Just moments after Emma sat down on a bench to try on the shoes, Joanna Schlabach, the mother of one of Miriam's students, sidled up to them. Miriam had noticed Joanna had been busy at the cash register helping a customer when they'd first walked in, but it seemed Joanna hadn't spotted them till now.

"It's nice to see you *maedels* out doing some shopping," she greeted them. "Those sneakers Emma is trying are 'buy one, get the second pair half off' till the end of the week," she informed Miriam.

"*Danke,*" Miriam replied. "But I don't know that she needs two pairs right now. The way she's growing, they may not fit by the time cooler weather comes along."

"*Verra* true. And anyway, I was thinking…" Joanna bent down to Emma's size. "You know my daughter Abby, don't you? She's two years older than you."

Emma nodded.

"I have some shoes of hers that she's outgrown. They may be too big for you now, but you can grow into them." Standing up, she switched her focus to Miriam. "When the school year starts again, I'll send them along with Abby to give to you. Although—" Joanna leaned closer, yet her voice didn't hush any "—who knows? Maybe you won't even be teaching by then."

She winked, and Miriam blinked. "I'm not sure what you mean, Joanna."

"What I mean is sometimes when it comes to matters of the heart, things can move *verra* quickly. By summer's end, you may have other plans—and other people—to keep you busy. Who knows if you'll be teaching? Why, the other day at worship everyone was noticing how comfortable you and Benjamin are together."

"Oh, well…" Her cheeks instantly heated, not because of what Joanna said as much as what she thought Emma might have heard. The child looked up and tilted her head, appearing confused. "Thank you for offering Abigail's shoes, Joanna." She sloughed off the woman's remark about love. "It's *verra* nice of you to think of Emma," she said.

Then bending over, she pinched the toe of Emma's trial shoe to make sure there was some, but not too much, room to grow. Satisfied, she looked up at Emma. "What do you think? Want to walk around a bit and see how they feel?"

As Emma tested out the sneakers, Joanna excused herself to check on another customer. Miriam kept her eye on the child and noted Emma's pleased expression when she came back to Miriam's side.

"You look like you like them."

"I do," Emma replied. "May I keep them on?"

"Absolutely."

As she placed Emma's old shoes in the box, she saw Emma's smile fading.

"Are you thinking you may want to try on another pair? If so, that's fine, Emma. We have time."

"No, I like these."

"Then what's bothering you, *liebling*? You can tell me."

Emma hesitated for a moment then said, "Did Abby's *mamm* say you may not be my teacher anymore?"

"Oh, Emma." This is exactly what she'd been afraid of when Joanna had gotten to yakking. "She was just talking, like people do sometimes. Not to worry about that, you hear?"

Yet, wasn't she doing the same thing? Talking just to be talking so she could cover up so many untruths.

"Now, let's pay for your shoes. Then we can take the sandwiches and iced tea we made to your *onkel* and his workers down at the restaurant. *Oll recht*?"

She knew that would divert Emma's thoughts for the time being. The child really had come to like her uncle very much and enjoyed helping him. At one point, Emma had even disclosed that Sarah told her that before Hannah married her *daed*, she'd been a big helper to him when her *mamm* went to be with the Lord. It seemed *Gott* had decided the two girls would grow up fast.

After leaving the Shoe Rack, ten minutes later, Miriam pulled her buggy up to the site of Benjamin's restaurant. After speaking to Henry Miller, it was agreed that Benjamin would receive a three-month suspension on the lease amount if he replaced the entire roof at his own expense. After discussing it with her, since the roof wasn't all that large, Benjamin had decided that was the best deal. Boxes of shingles had been delivered and were stacked up outside the restaurant, and he had hired a couple of friends to help with the project. What she didn't know, and what came as a surprise to her as she caught sight of the men on the roof, was that one of those helpers was her brother-in-law, Jeremiah. When had he come into the picture?

She was sure her mouth dropped open some as Benja-

min stood up on the roof and smiled. Looking pleased to
see them, he waved.

"We brought sandwiches." Emma held up one of their
lunch bags.

"Gut! Danke." He gave a thumbs up. "We'll finish up
this one section. Then we'll come inside to eat."

Just as she'd been surprised to see Jeremiah, she was
equally startled when she and Emma walked inside the restaurant. There, her sister was washing down tabletops while
her son, Aaron, sat in a stroller, gurgling and shaking a rat-
tling toy.

"I didn't know you were coming." Rebecca hailed her.
"What a nice surprise!"

"Jah, I'm surprised too," Miriam said.

"Looks like we had the same idea." Rebecca nodded
at the lunch totes in Miriam's and Emma's hands. Then
she motioned over her shoulder at the picnic basket she'd
brought.

"Jah, we thought the men would be hungry, and that we'd
do a little cleaning too. But I see you already got started
on that."

"I saw the baskets of rags and cleaning products in the
corner there. I hope it's okay I'm doing this."

"Jah, sure," Miriam answered, contradicting how confused she still felt seeing her sister and mostly Jeremiah
there, taking such an active part in Benjamin's business.
She was glad her discomfit didn't rub off on Emma though.
As soon as they set their bags next to the basket, Emma
wasn't shy about approaching Rebecca.

"May I play with Aaron?"

"He would love that, Emma."

Even amid the hammering noises going on overhead,
they could hear Emma talking to Aaron in a singsong voice

as she crouched next to him. Quick as a snap, Miriam's mood shifted. When it came to anything positive regarding the girl, there was no way she could hold back a smile.

Rebecca appeared touched by the scene as well. Laying aside her dirty cloth, she picked up a clean one to wipe her hands then scurried close to Miriam. "Emma's talking now!" she exclaimed, her eyes bright.

"It happened just the other day."

"Oh, Miriam, you're so good with *kinner*."

"It wasn't me." Miriam discounted the remark. "It was… well, it was funny is what it was." She chuckled. "Because Bumper—that's Emma's kid goat that she got when we went to Beachy's one day. And the goat…well, it got Benjamin's hat when he was showing us the kid's hoof and how things could get caught in there and—"

Her sister laid a hand on her shoulder to stop her. Rebecca looked baffled, and why wouldn't she be? Miriam knew she was doing a poor job of explaining. "Whatever happened, it sounds like you do well with both kid goats and *kinner*. You were always *gut* mothering me. And mothering isn't an easy job, ain't so? I don't know how you did it."

"Why, you seem to be a natural *mamm*, Rebecca. Motherhood suits you." She couldn't have been more truthful. Each time she saw her nephew Aaron, he looked to be healthy and content.

"I learned from the best," Rebecca replied. "From you, Miriam."

Suddenly, Rebecca reached out and hugged her.

Yes, for sure and certain, it was a day full of surprises. All at once, her sister's totally unexpected compliment and affection warmed her heart. Just as it had when Rebecca comforted her after her run-in with their mother at Aaron's party. Overwhelmed, she realized how much she'd been missing such a closeness with her sister. She'd let her awk-ward feelings about Jeremiah keep Rebecca at a distance. Taken aback, Miriam didn't know how to respond. "That's nice of you to say," she muttered.

"I only speak the truth. And I'm sure you and Benjamin couldn't be more pleased that Emma's doing better. I'm so happy for you two in more ways than one." She grinned. "And now look at us here together. Who would've ever thought it? I figured if Jeremiah is going to be a part of Benjamin's restaurant, then I need to be a part of it too."

Powerless to help herself, Miriam's brows shot up. Un-able to tamp down the old familiar feelings of exclusion from life around her, her stomach tightened.

"From the look on your face, I guess Benjamin didn't mention anything about Jeremiah."

"*Nee, nee*, he didn't."

"It was very last minute. I just found out this morning myself."

"Oh." That helped loosen her twisted insides some. But what should it matter anyway? Benjamin was under no ob-ligation to tell her everything, was he? Nor had she shared her history regarding Jeremiah with him, had she?

Besides, as she and Rebecca began sorting out sand-wiches on a clean table, she had to ask herself how many other people she'd been withholding the truth from about her and Benjamin. There was her sister to whom she hadn't disclosed a thing. Joanna Schlabach. Esther Klein. The list of townsfolk kept growing and growing and fooling them all wasn't something she was proud of.

But it was only for sweet Emma's sake, ain't so?

She glanced over at Emma, who was playing patty-cake with Aaron, which put her mind at ease some. That is, until minutes later when Benjamin came in the door with his buddies. She watched as he took off his new straw hat and wiped his sweaty brow. Even with his unkempt hair and smudged face, he was still a handsome sight to see. Glancing her way, all he had to do was smile and instantly her cheeks flushed. Her heart leapt involuntarily.

Leaving her to wonder that perhaps she wasn't being honest with someone else.

Herself.

"I lost again!"

It was well after suppertime when Benjamin tossed yet another handful of playing cards on the coffee table. Both Miriam and Emma, seated on the floor across from him, beamed at his defeat. "Are you sure you aren't stacking the deck somehow, Emma?" He playfully narrowed his eyes at his niece. "You always seem to win at Go Fish."

Emma giggled at his question. He was glad to see she knew he was only kidding.

"Tell your uncle you don't need to cheat to beat him at cards." Miriam laughed.

"I don't need to cheat to win, *Onkel* Benjamin. But maybe you do."

They all burst out laughing at Emma's smart comeback. To him, it seemed a good way to end the day.

"Well, I've had enough of you beating me for one night," he replied. "Time to get ready for bed, young one."

Emma groaned but promptly obeyed. As she rose from the floor, he spied cookie crumbs still stuck to the lap of her dress. "And don't forget to brush your teeth," he kindly reminded her. "You ate so many chocolate-chip cookies, I'm hoping you don't turn into one."

As Emma took off down the hall, Miriam gathered up the cards, placing them back in the box. Meanwhile, every one of his muscles ached and he took his time rising from the floor and settling onto the cozy couch.

"How can you have so much energy?" He yawned. "You've been working longer than I have today. You helped at the restaurant, then came back here and made dinner. Then you baked cookies with Emma and cleaned up the kitchen for the second time. And you don't seem a bit tired." In fact, even to his weary eyes, her deep blue eyes were as pretty as he'd ever seen. The sun had turned her cheeks a glowing pink and the way her—

Suddenly, he caught himself taking in her every feature and stopped.

Meanwhile, looking up from her spot on the floor, she gave him an impish grin. "Whereas you look as if you've aged ten years from your manual labor today."

He chuckled. "*Danke.* It's so kind of you to say so."

"You know I'm just teasing you. It looked like you got a decent section of the roof finished. That's a big job. It was fortunate you had some help."

"*Verra* true. I couldn't do it all by myself."

As she pushed her glasses up on her nose, he wasn't sure what to expect next.

"I knew you said Jonah Hershberger would be there today, but I was surprised to see Jeremiah."

For whatever reason, she sounded almost too nonchalant. But knowing Miriam as he did, that meant she wanted to be filled in without having to ask directly. He was happy to explain.

"I forgot to tell you that when I went to the home improvement store to order shingles the other day, Jeremiah was working. He asked if the roof here had a problem, and that's when I told him about the restaurant. He immediately offered to help, and I told him I already had hired

Jonah and his brother Noah. But when Noah backed out, I told Jeremiah, and he was thrilled to pitch in. More than helping with repairs, he wants to help open the restaurant."

"Oh, so that's why Rebecca said what she did." Miriam nodded. "He isn't happy at the store?"

Benjamin shrugged. "To him, it's something to fall back on if the restaurant doesn't work. He really wants to come aboard and take a chance with me."

"As a partner?" She blinked.

"*Nee, nee.* Maybe he could be an assistant manager someday. But time will tell."

"Hmm," she replied.

"That's all you have to say?"

"What else is there to say?" Her lips drew in tightly.

"You seem like that'd be a problem with you."

"I do? Why would you think that?"

Why was she getting so touchy? "I don't know, Miriam. I mean when we went to Aaron's birthday party, you mentioned issues with your *mamm*, but not with Rebecca and Jeremiah. I hope I didn't overstep or not consider you in some way," he said honestly.

"*Nee*, it's all fine. And, anyway, it's your restaurant."

"With many of your *gut* ideas being put into place."

"But with *Gott*'s help, you're the one who will make it successful, Benjamin."

"Now, that really is *verra* kind of you to say." He sighed, glad that her shoulders seemed to ease. Whatever she'd been pent up about appeared to have been put out into the open and brought to rest. "*Danke* again for all the cleaning you did today. You and Rebecca make quite a team."

"It was kind of nice." She placed her elbows on the table, cupping her chin in her hands. "It reminded me of when we were *kinner*, and she'd try to help me clean the house.

But then, things do change, don't they?" She sighed. "We both grew up, and she got married and has a house of her own now."

"You know, I remember when we were all young, I'd see Jeremiah come up your drive quite often. I really thought, being the same age, that you and he might wind up together," he said frankly. "But he and Rebecca are a far better match."

"They are a *gut* match. But are you saying I'm not good enough for a guy like him?" Her palms went flat against the wooden surface.

Why was she getting so defensive?

"Miriam, I'm not saying anything like that. If you ask me, after working with Jeremiah today and getting to know him better, I think you're too much for him." What he held back from saying was that the more he got to know her, the more he realized she was a far better woman than most men deserved.

"You mean I'm overbearing," she stated flatly.

"Well…" With a slight grin, he teetered his hand in the air, hoping the gesture would make her smile too.

She crossed her arms over her chest, apparently not thinking it was funny.

"My *schweschder* is cuter and sweeter. She always has been. Everyone thinks so. Even I do."

"You're trying to put words in my mouth that aren't there." As tired as he was, he still didn't want to see her upset. He scratched his forehead, thinking how to say what he meant. "Look, Miriam, Jeremiah might be a nice person, but he's not the sharpest tool in the shed. And just like I don't plan to make him a partner, I don't think he would've been a good one for you. You deserve a life partner who's your equal."

His eyes met hers as the word *partner* hung in the air between them. It was exactly what they had promised each other they'd pretend to be when they began their courtship. But instead of creating a sense of oneness between them, he saw her tense. She gazed up at him and bit her lip.

"You have something you want to say, don't you?"

"How do you know?"

"Because I know you." Better than any woman he'd ever known, he realized.

"*Nee*, it can wait." She shook her head. "It's been a long day, and you may be too tired to hear it."

"That bad, huh?" His jaw clenched.

"Not bad. I just need some help, that's all."

"Miriam, I'll do anything to help you." He held out his hands to her. "I hope you know that."

"Well, then…" Rising to her feet, she came to sit next to him on the sofa. So close, he could see the worry lines around her eyes. "Benjamin, I, uh… I'd like for you to go see the bishop with me."

"Bishop Gingerich?" He straightened. "I don't understand."

"Neither do I," she said, sounding as perplexed as he felt. "I know I said I'd do this courting thing with you, and it's not like I want to stop. I want the best for Emma. But my conscience lately… I don't know." Her shoulders went limp. "Esther and her *mamm* were amazed by our courtship. What happens to their faith when they learn we're not really a couple? Joanna Schlabach today…she said things in front of Emma about me possibly not teaching soon. Then there's my sister and so many others in town…" She pursed her lips. "And it's not as if I don't love Emma and want to care for her, but—"

"You feel guilty in a way?"

"I do, and I don't want Emma to get hurt. I just…need to talk to the bishop and sort of cleanse myself?" The statement ended with a question. "I need to tell one person the truth about us."

It was strange she was saying this, because recently he'd been feeling that boundary lines were blurring. Even he wasn't sure what was real and what was false lately.

Before they could say more, Emma stepped into the room. "I'm ready for bed now. Will you come say prayers?" She looked at him then at Miriam. "Both of you?"

He and Miriam stood at the same time, ready to follow behind Emma, but his niece didn't move. Reaching out, she took his right hand and joined it with Miriam's left. He didn't mind the affectionate gesture at all. In fact, Miriam's hand felt warm and right in his grasp. But as Emma skittered ahead of them down the hallway, a chill ran through him. When Lizzie and Roman were alive, he remembered seeing them walking the same way each evening, hand in hand behind their daughter all the way to her bedroom.

His grasp loosened as his chest tightened. Once again, Miriam was probably right. Perhaps it was time to pay the bishop a visit after all.

Chapter Ten

A few evenings later, Miriam stood beside Benjamin on Bishop Gingerich's doorstep, clenching her hands nervously, wondering why she'd ever suggested they come see the bishop. She'd never been one for opening up to others much, so what had she been thinking?

But then, curiously, as she was about to let the idea die down, Benjamin had been the one to insist they arrange a visit once he and his buddies got the roofing job completed. And now here they were. They hadn't had to travel far to reach their destination after dropping off Emma at Rebecca's, which was both good and bad. Miriam would've liked Joy to keep trotting off into the sunset.

Taking a deep breath, she looked over at Benjamin. "Are you going to knock? Or am I?" she whispered.

His left brow rose. "Does it matter?"

"I didn't know if who did what would set our tone for the rest of the evening."

"I believe you're overthinking this." His gave her a slight smile and when she didn't smile back, he squeezed her hand. "It's going to be all right, Miriam. We're in this together, remember? And I'm happy to do the knocking."

The warmth of his hand helped, along with his soothing comments. "*Nee.* This was my idea. I'll knock." Straightening her shoulders, she rapped on the door a little too forcefully.

Yet when Rachel Gingerich came to answer the door, the bishop's daughter didn't appear the least bit annoyed. Unfortunately, she looked as stunning as ever. Miriam inwardly groaned as Rachel turned her eyes on Benjamin.

"I know you're not here to see me." She fluttered her lashes at him. "My *daed* said you'd be coming and asked me to get the door since my *mamm* is at her sister's. Come on in." She crooked a finger for them to follow her. "*Daed*'s out back."

Miriam's heartbeat turned to a rapid pace as Rachel led them through the house and out onto the back deck. The colorful beauty of purple irises, pink phlox and black-eyed Susans surrounding the wooden porch did help soothe her nerves some. So did the bishop's warm welcome when he laid aside his Bible on a small patio table and stood up from his Adirondack chair to greet them.

"Hello. *Wilkumme. Gut* to see you both. Have a seat, you two."

He directed them to the pair of matching outdoor chairs sitting across from his. Before he got reseated, he thanked Rachel and waved to dismiss her, fortunately. Miriam didn't recall ever being in such tight quarters with the man they called Bishop. Somehow, so close in his presence, the lines around his sky-blue eyes appeared to be more from fifty or so years of joyful living rather than seriousness.

"*Danke* for letting us come," Benjamin started.

"I'm glad you did. I hope you don't mind sitting outside. But it seemed a mighty good evening for it. Not too hot for this time of year."

"That's true," she said in a hushed voice.

"But you didn't come to talk about the weather this summer, ain't so? What can I help you with?" He settled into his chair and stroked his gray-tinted beard that fell nearly past the first two buttons on his shirt, appearing ready to listen.

She and Benjamin glanced at one another. Benjamin opened his mouth, but nothing came out. She completely understood. Her mind was a jumble of thoughts, yet she had no idea what to say first.

Finally, the bishop broke their silence. "Neither of you have to be uncomfortable around me," he told them. "I may be the bishop, but I'm just a man, remember? I work at a job to earn a living, just like you, and I only became the bishop because of the lot that was drawn." He leaned forward in his chair and held out his hands. "I know it's hard sometimes for a person to know where to start when they come to me, but I find the truth is a *gut* place."

"The truth, *jah*." She noticed Benjamin's jaw tighten as he repeated the word. "Well, the truth is, Bishop, I received a letter from my brother in Boston. You remember Stephen? My *Englischer* brother?"

"*Jah*, I saw him when he was in town after the accident," Bishop Gingerich replied solemnly.

Benjamin nodded. "After he left, he wrote to me, saying that he and his wife were going out of the country on business, but once that job ended, they wanted to come to take Emma to live with them up east in Boston. He said it'd be better for her because there's two of them, and they make a very *gut* living. And, well…" Miriam had watched him nervously twirl his hat in his hand the entire time he spoke. But then he stopped and sighed. "I didn't believe that's what Lizzie and Roman would want for their daughter, my niece, so I… I…"

She didn't think she'd ever seen Benjamin look so uncomfortable. Feeling badly for him, she stepped in. "So, he approached me. He came to my house with a beautiful bouquet of flowers."

"Flowers, eh? Very gentlemanly of you." A smile twitched at the bishop's mouth as he glanced at Benjamin, which seemed to relax him a bit. Seeing the bishop's slight grin and recalling the sight of Benjamin on her doorstep, her anxiety slackened too. Until the bishop turned to her again.

"And then what happened?" he asked.

"Oh, um…well…" She folded her hands together to keep from wringing them. "Then Benjamin asked if he could court me so that Stephen would think he had someone in mind to possibly marry and help with Emma. And—" she raised a finger in the air "—he thought it best if it was someone that he didn't have to be concerned about romantically. That way he could concentrate on caring for Emma while figuring out how to make a living."

"And you were *oll recht* with that?" Bishop Gingerich arched a brow.

"Not at all," Benjamin blurted out. "At first she said no."

"I did at that. I thought he was *verrickt.* Crazy." She chuckled, feeling more at ease. "Especially at the idea of the two of us courting. Who would believe that?"

The bishop's forehead furrowed. "Why is that?"

"Because…" She started to say the reason she'd always had in mind about how different they were. He was popular, she was nearly a social outcast. He was better looking than most men in town. No one noticed her behind her glasses. And yet, while all of that was true at face value, the more she'd gotten to know him, were they really *so* different?

While she grappled with what to say, Benjamin replied. "Miriam is stable, and I'm the one who's been here then gone and then back again. Also, she was born smart, and I'm a learn-as-I-go kind of person."

She blinked at him, surprised by his flattering view of her.

Benjamin continued. "For as long as we've lived next door to each other, we've never gotten to truly know one another. But, thankfully, Miriam knew Emma better than I did from being close friends with Lizzie and Roman and also being my niece's teacher. When Emma went missing—"

"I never heard anything about that," the bishop interrupted.

"That's because she wasn't missing for long. But long enough to be frightening." Benjamin's eyes widened. "As it turned out, she was at the far rear of our properties on a seated tree swing that Roman had built for her birthday. Miriam thought she might be there because Roman and Lizzie used to sit on that swing with her. But I had no clue about it, and Miriam led me there."

"While I kept repeating Psalm 23 in my head."

Bishop Gingerich shot her an amused but quizzical look.

"I don't know why I added that." Shaking her head, her face flushed.

"But after that happened," Benjamin went on, "I thought maybe I wouldn't be good at parenting Emma since she'd gone missing on my watch."

"*Jah*, but at that point, I thought just the opposite." Miriam jumped in just as she had that same day. "Seeing Emma in that swing, it was obvious that she shouldn't leave Sugarcreek. I thought it would be more healing for her to stay here to be close to her *mamm* and *daed*'s memories."

"I can see why both of you were thinking the way you were." The bishop nodded. "So, what changed? What brought you two together?"

"Well, Miriam told me what she thought was best for Emma. And, let's just say, she can be very forthright and outspoken." She'd heard the same thing said about her before, but Benjamin's tone was appreciative rather than accusatory. Looking at her, his eyes were warm, which made her heart feel the same. "So then…" He nodded for her to continue.

Clearing her throat, she went on. "So then I, uh, I told him he could ask me to walk out with him again if he wanted to."

"And when I did, she said yes."

"That's the part of your story that I've heard," Bishop Gingerich said.

"You have?" they asked in unison.

"*Jah*. You two are big news, from what I understand. If you meant for your courtship to be out in the open, what you've done has worked well."

"That's exactly what we've been finding out." Miriam spoke up. "But now we—me, mostly… I'm feeling badly because other *maedels* who haven't found someone to court are looking at us, and they're seeing the two of us together as a sort of wondrous thing. It's giving them hope."

"Do you think hope is a bad thing?" the bishop asked.

"*Nee*, but…" She scrunched her forehead, knowing hope was good and right. But still, she couldn't stop stewing. False hope was wrong, wasn't it?

Benjamin spoke up, interrupting her thoughts. "I think what Miriam's trying to say is that we started out our courtship with a falsehood, and she's not feeling good about that."

"*Jah,* you did," Bishop Gingerich replied. "You started out courting with a story you made up, but you also started it with love, ain't so?"

Love? Had the bishop really said that? Her cheeks flamed.

One look at Benjamin and she could tell from his shocked expression the word had rattled him too. Still, in a strange way, he seemed tickled. He even laughed. "Well, I wouldn't describe it as love," Benjamin piped up. "And you wouldn't, either, Bishop, if you saw how Miriam nearly slammed her front door in my face when I came asking her to court me that morning."

"That's right." She chuckled, glad Benjamin had chosen to lighten the conversation. "I handed those roses right back to you, didn't I?" She glanced at him.

"More like you smashed them into my chest."

"And then remember how you admitted I was right and that some of the roses were mine?" She grinned.

"I should've known I couldn't fool you."

Absorbed in their shared memory from that day, they broke into a fit of laughter. It was moments before they caught themselves and turned back to the bishop.

She winced. "Sorry about that."

"No need to be sorry." The bishop smiled. "But when I said 'love,' I meant you both began your relationship because of your combined love for Emma."

"Oh, *jah*. Emma. Definitely." Benjamin shifted in his chair.

"For sure and certain," Miriam agreed, smoothing her skirt.

"Many couples start out with a lot less," he told them. "To my way of thinking, courting is simply a process where a man and woman get to know each other. Some couples even start out with lies, lying to themselves that they've found the one person *Gott* intended for them."

Benjamin nodded, and she knew he'd experienced what the bishop was saying.

"Being a parent myself, I can't fault you for what you've done on Emma's behalf," Bishop Gingerich continued. "Both your hearts are in the right place when it comes to Emma and what you deem is best for her. I don't know how long it will last, and I doubt you two do either. Again, that's what courting is all about. But—" he looked directly at Benjamin "—I do tend to agree that Roman and Lizzie would also have wanted their daughter to be in familiar surroundings with two people she can feel secure with.

"The other thing is…" Bishop Gingerich cast his eyes on her. "As far as being concerned about giving people false hope, Miriam, I believe that's their issue, not yours."

"You do?"

"*Jah*. They should be putting their hope in *Gott*, not in a couple who's courting, don't you think? And I would also say—"

Suddenly there was a loud crashing sound from the open window behind where the bishop was sitting.

Miriam jumped in her seat. But the bishop didn't bother to turn to look.

"I'm sure it's Zeke, our cat. He has a bad habit of being nosy and leaping up on the bookshelf underneath that window," he explained. "He probably knocked over a book or two."

Curious, Miriam peered through the screen but couldn't see the bishop's pet or any movement. Benjamin seemed totally uninterested, focusing on the bishop.

"You were going to say something else, Bishop?" he inquired.

"Oh, *jah*." The bishop held up a finger. "Keep praying *Gott* will make the best of this situation for Emma. And, in the meantime, who knows? You may be thinking wrong. Maybe why I—I mean others—are believing in you two as a couple is because what they're seeing between you doesn't look false at all."

Miriam was so stunned by the bishop's words that she could barely get out of her chair to leave. She'd arrived there imagining she and Benjamin would be reprimanded for what they'd done. Instead, she felt encouraged. And while that was a good thing, as she and Benjamin walked side by side out to the buggy, what the bishop described between them, she was feeling too. She wasn't sure what to think about that. Was it good or bad?

Seated beside him in the buggy, Benjamin thought Miriam looked to be glowing like the golden rays in the evening sky as he steered Joy over the road toward home. Her natural beauty seemed more intensified even in the subtle light. The slender chin of hers, usually set in iron determination, was lifted up to search his face, appreciation gleaming in her deep blue eyes.

"Thank you for going to see Bishop Gingerich this evening, Benjamin. I do feel better now."

He could tell there was a certain degree of contentment about her. Just as she could also take one look at him and sense his discomfort.

"Is something wrong?" she asked.

"No, why?" He returned his focus to the road, not daring to glance at her as he fibbed.

"You don't seem as relieved as I am after seeing the bishop. I feel like an ox yoke has been lifted from my shoulders. Or is it that you're hungry? You didn't eat much dinner. Is that it? There's still plenty of leftovers back at your house," she offered.

His stomach was churning, but not from hunger.

"Miriam…"

"What?"

Looking over at her, one by one, he watched each of her lovely features become shadowed. It pained him to see her that way. Lately, as surprising as it was to him, he cared too much for her to want anything less than happiness lighting her eyes.

But the time had come, hadn't it?

"Benjamin!" She shouted his name and grabbed his arm. "Look out!"

Instantly, his eyes met the road. In a flash, he jerked the reins, steering Joy away from an Amish man on a bicycle.

Once past the rider, Miriam spoke up. "You need to pull over and tell me what's going on with you," she demanded.

Again, his insides tightened, knowing she was right. He let Joy walk a few more yards until he spotted safe, even ground to guide her on to. As he brought the horse to a halt, the thumping in his chest sped up.

A chorus of crickets were chirping all around the buggy, but not loud enough to drown out what he needed to say. Turning to face Miriam, again he noticed the glow had faded from her cheeks. Guilt stabbed at him. "There's something I've been meaning to tell you," he said apologetically.

"Oh, *jah*? Meaning to tell me or meaning to let whatever it is go unsaid until your conscience couldn't take it anymore?"

She knew him well, didn't she?

"Promise you won't hate me?"

"Do I seem like a woman who would make a promise she may not be able to keep?" She raised her brows.

No, she wasn't that for sure.

"It's nothing awful, Miriam. Honest. It's just that I didn't say everything there was to say to the bishop. But then, I didn't think this particular thing was something he needed to know."

"I hate when you talk in riddles."

"You're right. I'm sorry. What happened is…" He paused, rubbing his forehead. "Well, a few days after I let Stephen know that we were courting, he contacted me before he and Angie left the country. He said Angie was concerned that I'd never had a long-lasting relationship before, so why would courting you be any different?"

"I can see her point."

"Me too. That's why I did what I did."

"Which was?"

"I stretched the truth."

"How so?"

"I told him that we hadn't mentioned it to anyone else, but that we were…" He hesitated.

Miriam lowered her head, peering over her glasses. "We were what?"

"Engaged." He smiled, hoping she would too.

"Engaged?" She gasped. "Benjamin, how could you? This partnership of ours is getting too out of hand."

"No, it isn't. Don't you see? I told Stephen we are getting married August fifteenth."

"You actually set a date?" Her jaw dropped. "That's coming up quickly."

"Right, and Stephen and Angie will still be out of the country, so they'll have no idea that the wedding never happened."

He'd rarely witnessed Miriam speechless. But she was. She blinked.

"Are you *oll recht*?" He laid a hand over hers. Still, she said nothing, so he blabbered on. "Miriam, you look worried. But you needn't be. This will all blow over. It's nothing to be concerned about."

The look she gave him was skeptical to say the least. "I hope you're right." She shook her head. "I can't believe you kept this quiet. Why didn't you tell me this a long time ago?"

"I didn't want you to worry," he said sincerely.

"So, it's better that I'm worried now?"

He ducked his head. "No, it's not."

"Benjamin." She sought his eyes, speaking his name firmly.

"Yeah?" He met her gaze.

"Don't ever hold back on me like that again."

"I won't. I promise," he said fervently, wanting to be a man she could trust.

Taking up the reins, as soon as Joy's hooves hit the pavement again, he stole a glance at the woman sitting beside him. The Miriam he used to know would have likely scolded him for less. Even earlier, on the bishop's deck, recalling their first encounter with each other, seemed like something that had happened forever ago. They'd been through so much together since then. Miriam had become his closest confidante. A beautiful companion he could depend on and laugh with. A cherished person in his and Emma's life. A person he wanted to share time with.

Yes, Miriam *Shock* appeared to have changed so much. But the question niggled at him. Had he changed, too, since he'd gotten to know her?

Chapter Eleven

❦

"*Danke* for making this dress for me. I like this blue color lots."

Standing in the Byler kitchen, Miriam's heart swelled, seeing the happy look on Emma's face. Throughout the morning, she'd gotten the impression Emma was somewhat anxious about going to the picnic Hannah Burkholder had invited them to. That made sense being that Emma hadn't been around a large group of children much in the past few months. But it was evident from the way her eyes were sparkling now that Emma was also excited about the event. Whereas, Miriam was just plain apprehensive. Not that she'd ever let Emma know how she was feeling.

"You're *verra* welcome, *liebling*," she replied brightly. "I'm glad you like it, and I'm happy to make you more. You're growing so tall, like the sunflowers that are about ready to bloom this season. Although, you're way prettier," she added, causing Emma to smile even more. "And with that blonde hair of yours, you can wear any color."

Emma had asked for help getting her hair brushed and pulled into a bun. Even though Miriam knew Emma could manage the task herself, she could also see that Emma wanted a maternal touch at times. Happy to oblige, Miriam had done more than a simple bun. She'd braided Emma's hair, like she used to do for Rebecca when she was a young girl, and pinned it to the back of Emma's head. Now in her *kapp* and wearing her new sneakers, Miriam gave Emma the once-over. "My, you look like a young *maedel* who is ready for a picnic, Emma."

"I do?" Emma asked.

"*Jah,* you do." Miriam bobbed her head affirmatively.

"I'm glad you're the one taking me," Emma replied. "Sarah said her *mamm* invited other *kinner* from school. She told me all about it at worship."

Oh, yes! Worship!

After she and Benjamin had visited with Bishop Gingerich, she'd been more comfortable about their partnership. And even though Benjamin had surprised her that night on the ride home with the secret of their "engagement," hard as it was, she'd managed to curb her distrustful nature. She wanted to believe he'd never hold anything back from her again. Together with Emma, the three of them had settled into an easy daily rhythm once more. Life was back on an even keel. That is, until Sunday's worship at the Klingers'. Then everything had fallen off balance again.

As soon as she had entered the Klingers' barn with Benjamin and Emma, she'd noticed some raised eyebrows. Those brows, however, hadn't seemed curved upward with curiosity, but more like arched with disapproval. As the day went on, she could tell she was right. For whatever reason, the women hadn't exactly shunned her when she went to sit on their side of the barn, but they hadn't been openly welcoming her either. And when she'd tried to help the ladies serve lunch after the church service, she'd gotten the impression they'd been attempting to keep her at arm's length. It was puzzling, because that even included women who'd reached out to her recently, happy about the courtship.

That evening, after Emma was in bed, she'd told Benjamin what she'd experienced. He'd listened kindly and intently to all she had to say. And while he hadn't shrugged his shoulders like she'd seen other men do to squelch their mate's concerns, he hadn't been at all perturbed. He'd suggested that maybe the newness of their courting had simply worn off with townsfolk. And that wasn't a bad thing, was it? he'd asked.

Working to push aside what had happened days before, she smiled at Emma. "I suppose we should get going. Would you like to be in charge of the basket of brownies we made for the picnic?"

"Jah!" Emma eagerly went to grab the basket from the counter just as Benjamin entered the kitchen.

"May I have one of those?" He eyed their dessert.

Emma held the basket close, looking to Miriam for permission.

"Just one." As Miriam held up a single digit, Benjamin grabbed the largest in the pile.

Taking a huge bite, he rubbed his belly. "Delicious!" he said, causing Emma to beam. "You two have a *wunderbaar* time picnicking while I'm at the restaurant working on repairs."

"Oh, we will have fun, won't we, Emma?" Miriam winked at the girl.

"Uh-huh." Emma giggled. "Maybe we'll have a brownie left to bring home."

"For me?" Benjamin's face lit up.

"Nee," Emma said. "For Bumper."

The child had been catching on how to tease her uncle, which warmed Miriam's heart. It reminded her of how things had been light and fun between Emma and her parents.

"I should've known." Benjamin sighed before popping the remaining morsel in his mouth.

Looking at him, Miriam hoped he was right about the ill feelings she'd sensed at worship. But she doubted it with all her heart since her instincts were usually on target. But then, how could she expect Benjamin to relate? He'd always been welcomed in every social situation. And why wouldn't he be? Even now, ready to go do repair work in his rumpled shirt and paint-stained pants, he looked as cute as he did when he was cleaned up for Church Sundays. Like a man of strength and integrity that any woman would want to be married to.

She flushed at the thought and tried to push her observation out of her mind. Although, it wasn't easy. Especially when right before she and Emma were about to walk out the door, Benjamin leaned close. How could she ignore his subtle smile and those caring blue eyes of his?

"*Danke* for being so sweet and taking her today," he whispered. "I hope it goes well for you."

"*Jah*, it'll be fine."

She'd said the words easily and assuredly, putting on an act to ease his worry. Yet all the way to Hannah's house, she was bracing herself for the worst. Having the women ignore her at worship felt as isolating as it always had. But she'd survive as she always had. If, however, their standoffish attitude affected Emma, that wouldn't be all right. She'd do anything to protect the child.

Ten minutes later, as she steered her buggy into Hannah's drive, right away she spotted a handful of women and twice as many children dotting the Burkholders' backyard. The women were all mothers she knew from school. They sat at picnic tables covered with checkered cloths laden with snacks. Meanwhile, the children were off playing games under the sun, working up their appetites. All of it should've been a delightful sight, yet Miriam's stomach tightened even more when they turned to look at her. Fortunately, after she and Emma parked and exited the buggy, Hannah and Sarah came running up to them.

Surprisingly, Hannah hugged Miriam tightly as if they were close-knit sisters. "Don't look shocked about anything I do or say, you hear?" Hannah whispered in her ear.

Taken back, Miriam quietly replied, "Okay."

After Hannah thanked Emma for the brownies and sent the girls off to play, she looped her free arm through Miriam's. Waving to the other ladies who were staring at them, she spoke loudly. "My *gut* friend here is going to help me fetch the hot dogs and iced tea. We'll be right out."

Once inside the Burkholder kitchen, Hannah took a quick glance out the back window before she began to explain.

"First off, Miriam, you need to know I'm on your side, no matter what. But here's the thing. Rachel Gingerich…" She shook her head before saying more. "She's being her usual nosy self and spreading rumors. She's saying you and Benjamin only started courting each other for Emma's sake. And what you're doing doesn't count as true courting because it's all a scheme."

"Oh, my…" Miriam's knees nearly buckled. "It wasn't the cat near the bookcase, it was Rachel."

Hannah gave her a confused look.

"Benjamin and I went to see the bishop about our circumstances, and she must've eavesdropped."

"That sounds like her." Hannah rolled her eyes. "Look, I don't care what brought you and Benjamin together. If you two only began courting for Emma, it's working for that little girl's sake who's lost so much."

Hearing such openness from Hannah, mixed emotions overwhelmed her. It only seemed right to be just as frank. "Honestly, Hannah, Benjamin's *Englischer* brother wanted to come and get Emma to take her to live in Boston because Benjamin didn't have a wife or a job. But we thought—"

Hannah held up a hand. "Say no more. I'm sure you both wanted her to be here at home to heal. I can relate to that, believe me. And anyway, in my opinion, you and Benjamin aren't pretending as much as you may think you are," she said with raised brows.

"What do you mean?" Miriam frowned.

"Just that seeing you both in town and at worship, there's an undeniable connection between you two."

Miriam's cheeks instantly heated. It was nice to hear people say such a thing. Except, the more she heard it, the more she wanted it to be true. "We try to put on a good act."

Hannah giggled. "Miriam, I used to be the town's matchmaker, remember? Nine times out of ten, I know a good thing when I see it. Make that nine and a half times."

Miriam started to smile then stopped. "So, *that's* why everyone started to pull back from me again on Church Sunday? Do they think I'm only courting Benjamin so I can claim that the most popular man in town is my beau? Did Rachel mention about Stephen's coming to get Emma too?"

"I'm not sure how much Rachel said. When the ladies started to talk about it, I shut them down, saying we shouldn't be gossiping. But whatever they've heard and think, I'm aiming to steer them straight." She began to gather up trays of hot dogs and buns. "Not only that, I plan to get them feeling bad about how they're thinking. Just you wait and see." She gave Miriam a conspiratorial wink. "Now, want to grab those pitchers of tea? The glasses are already outside."

Overwhelmed by Hannah's kindness, guilt rose inside her. She caught Hannah's arm. "Before we go outside, I need to apologize for that time you had me come here to talk to Sarah. Even though it was three years ago and before you and Jake were married, I still wish I hadn't acted so—"

Miriam shook her head, recalling how awful she'd behaved. She'd conducted herself poorly because, just hours before her visit, that was when Jeremiah had shattered her heart to pieces. After all the years of him hanging around the Schrock house, she was sure it was because one day the two of them would end up married for a lifetime. When he'd arrived at school that day during her lunchbreak, over-the-top excited, she thought he was there to profess his love for her. Instead, he told Miriam he was going to ask Rebecca to court him, leaving her completely devastated. Now it all seemed so foolish that she'd harbored so much anger and resentment. As Benjamin had said, Jeremiah wasn't her match. How she felt about Benjamin was proof of that.

As much as she thought she should share that, Hannah's hand flew up to stop her. "I could apologize for that day, too, Miriam. I was guarding my heart from Jake, trying to get you and others to help me escape love. But you can't help who you love, I've learned," she said with a shrug. "Still, the past is past, and today is a new day. So, put a smile on your face, and let's go remind the ladies of what we've all done for those who come into our hearts."

For sure and certain, she didn't know what Hannah was up to. But carrying the pitchers of iced tea alongside her prompted a prayer of gratitude to well up inside her. She hadn't had a friend who'd cared so much since Lizzie. *Gott* always knew how to help, didn't He? Even when she wasn't wise enough to ask Him.

The chatting ceased the moment she and Hannah reached

the picnic tables. After setting down the trays of food and pitchers, however, it appeared Hannah had much to say.

"Just look at those *kinner* out there having such a *gut* time!" she exclaimed. "It warms your heart, ain't so?" She turned her gaze from the children to their mothers. "Oh! And look at the goodies you all made. Frieda, I recognize your yummy lime Jell-O salad. And, Clara, I see you brought your *wunderbaar* macaroni salad. Ah, and no one makes baked beans as tasty as you do, Joanna. Plus, the apple fritters from you, Amanda, and granola bars you made, Laura, all look delicious. Are these foods that your *kinner* like?"

Miriam watched each mother nod before Hannah clapped her hands together. "Isn't it amazing how *Gott* made us women? What we won't do because of our love for a child, *jah*?"

With smiles all around, the ladies nodded again.

"You mean like being up every hour of the night with a baby who's teething?" Amanda glanced at her snoozing child in the stroller next to her. "And now he's sleeping soundly." She chuckled.

"I remember those days," Joanna chimed in.

Miriam noticed how Hannah let the grinning women trade teething stories for a few minutes before speaking again.

"Frieda, I'm still amazed at how you took in your sister's triplets when she went to be with the Lord. It couldn't have been easy with four children of your own."

"*Gott*'s been good to us," Frieda replied. "In a way, you've done the same with Jake's *kinner*, Hannah."

"*Jah,* it's unbelievable how you can so easily love a child like your own," Hannah replied. "And how many prayers you'll say and lengths you'll go to so a child can be healed. Like you did for your adopted son, Laura. And look at him now, out there running like the wind. But then, we women tend to do whatever we feel in our hearts is best for a child, don't we? We try to make a home for them, heal them and love them in every way we can. At least, I know that's what you ladies would do. All you ladies." She turned her eyes on Miriam, which led the mothers to do the same. In the silence that stood between them and her, Miriam was sure the temperature had risen to triple digits.

"Miriam, you've got to be so pleased Emma is talking now." Clara spoke up. "That child has been through a lot. She must feel comforted by you and Benjamin."

"That's what we hope," Miriam replied.

"And when it comes right down to it, it would be *verra gut* if Emma did get to stay in Sugarcreek," Joanna chimed in.

"*Jah,* we think so too," Miriam said. "We believe being here around folks who care about her and who she knows, like you all, would be best."

"And who better to help her than a teacher?" Frieda smiled. "Just like you taught us a thing or two about Noah. Here we thought he had a problem reading, and as it turned out, he just needed glasses."

Everyone laughed at that and even began lauding Miriam. It was nothing she was used to, and she took it all at face value considering the situation.

"Miriam, I was telling the *mamms* earlier that we're celebrating Abigail's birthday next weekend," Joanna said. "I hope you and Benjamin and Emma will come."

"*Danke.* We'd like to."

Glancing over at Hannah, who was all smiles, Miriam nodded her thanks. Relieved, she couldn't stop grinning herself as Hannah called the children to come eat. But once everyone settled in, for some reason Benjamin's confession about the lie he'd told his brother flashed through her mind. Right now, these women and others they might convince may be okay with her courting Benjamin for Emma's sake. But a real marriage for her and him? That would be debatable and probably laughable to them.

Honestly, as much as that realization caused a sad tug on her heart, weren't the two of them still an unlikely fit in her mind too?

Benjamin rolled the cream-colored paint over the far wall of the soon-to-be dining area, mindless of what he was doing. Instead, all his thoughts were focused on Miriam. Before she and Emma had left that morning, he'd almost blurted out that he'd be looking forward to seeing his two favorite girls soon. But then he'd stopped himself, realizing that he wasn't playing a part anymore. These days Emma and Miriam truly were his favorite things in life. Being with them was what made him feel complete. Emma was so easy to love and enjoy. And Miriam? How had his feelings for her gone beyond anything he'd ever imagined, beyond anything he'd ever felt for another woman? And what was he going to do, how traumatic was it going to be, when she was ready to get back to her real life?

Suddenly his musing was interrupted by a knock on the door. Had he accidentally locked Jeremiah out? Laying down the roller in the paint pan, he wiped his hands on his pants as he nonchalantly approached the door. Yet as soon as he saw the person on the other side of the glass, he stiffened. Roy Caldwell stood there, a man he wanted to be locked out of his life forever.

Opening the door, he could hardly speak through his clenched jaws. "Mr. Caldwell?"

"Benjamin, may I come in?"

Reluctantly, he held the entry open for Ethan's father, his mind racing. What in the world was this man doing here?

"I hope I'm not disturbing you," Mr. Caldwell told him. "I thought you might be here. I heard you're getting things ready to open a BBQ wings and rings restaurant."

"You did?"

"Nothing stays much of a secret in this town." Mr. Caldwell gave a wry smile. As the owner of the brick company that employed Amish and *Englischers*, Benjamin was sure the man heard plenty. "Anyway, how are you doing?"

Benjamin wasn't sure if he meant how he was doing with the restaurant repairs or with missing his brother and sister-in-law.

"I'm keeping busy," he uttered noncommittedly.

"I can see that." Ethan's father took a quick glance around the place. "I won't take a lot of your time. I simply wanted to thank you again for not, um…for not trying to press charges against Ethan. I mean, even though it was an accident, I appreciate you not trying to make things harder for him than they have been."

Hard for the boy? Really? He crossed his arms over his chest.

"I saw him with his baseball buddies recently."

"Yes, some days are better for him than others." Mr. Caldwell's voice softened as he dipped his head. "Thankfully, he's seeing a therapist, which helps. Anyway—" Ethan's father looked up at him "—when I heard you were opening a restaurant, I thought maybe I could say 'thank you' by giving you a small donation. Starting up a business can be costly. At least, it was for me twenty years ago."

"Mr. Caldwell." Benjamin held up a hand. "That's not necessary. I have the funds."

"Well, if you run into unexpected expenses, feel free to contact me."

"Again, not necessary," Benjamin said firmly, wishing the man would just leave. Thankfully, Jeremiah walked in the door carrying a sack of tools, interrupting the strained conversation.

"All right, I'll let you men get to work." Mr. Caldwell nodded. "But if you ever need anything in the future…"

"Danke." Benjamin feigned politeness while his insides seethed. What he needed, namely the family he'd lost, the man couldn't give him.

Chapter Twelve

Miriam tried to keep her focus on the burgers she was frying, but it wasn't easy with Benjamin on the other side of her small kitchen, replacing a curtain rod. It wasn't something she had asked him to do. Nor had she prompted him to fix the hinge on her back door. But when he'd shown up at her house with his toolbox a couple of hours after she got back from Hannah's picnic, she hadn't minded. Since Hannah's invitation to the picnic had included Emma spending the night—with Benjamin's approval—admittedly Miriam had felt a bit lost coming home alone. She was so accustomed—maybe too accustomed now that she thought about it—to spending her evenings with the young girl and her sweet uncle. She wondered if maybe Benjamin was at a loss, too. Perhaps that's why he'd come by. No doubt he'd already done enough repair work for the day and didn't need to do more.

Whatever his reason, the easiest way to keep her mind off his masculine presence in her modest home was to keep talking. And she'd done plenty of that since he'd arrived, relaying everything that had taken place at the picnic.

"Didn't I tell you that Rachel Gingerich likes to stir things up?" He glanced at her while his muscled arm reached to hold a bracket in place over her window frame.

"For sure and certain, you said that about her. I guess that means I should listen to you more often. But then…" She placed a free hand on her hip. "Maybe you should listen to me more, too, since I mentioned how odd the ladies had been acting. You thought I was overthinking things."

"I wasn't right about that, was I?"

"*Nee*, you weren't."

"But there is something I can always and forever be right about."

"Jah?" She gave him a quizzical look.

"I will never get the last word in with you, will I?"

"Not if I can help it!" She laughed and he did too.

Then, with a satisfactory smile etching his face, he began screwing in the remaining bracket. Finishing that, he picked up her sheer white curtain from where it was draped over a kitchen chair and, holding the rod, began to fuss with both. Right away, it was obvious he was much better with screws and nails than with thin material. Laying aside the spatula, she quickly joined him by the window.

"How about you hold the rod and I'll slip on the curtain," she offered.

The sun was still glowing through the windowpane, making his eyes shine even more than usual as he held the rod against his broad chest. Being so close to him made the simple task of finding the opening at the top of the curtain and sliding it over the rod very challenging. Finally, she managed and swiftly relinquished the curtain rod to him, rushing back to her sheltered spot at the stove.

"It's so hot in here." Wiping her brow with the back of her hand, she knew the warmth wasn't solely coming from her stovetop. "I should've cooked the burgers out on the grill."

"We can eat outside," Benjamin suggested. "It may be

cooler. That is, if you don't mind two picnics in the same day."

"I would like that *verra* much," she replied. Anything to get out from the confines of the space they were sharing. It felt way smaller without Emma there acting as a buffer between them.

As she finished cooking the burgers and dressing the buns with tomato slices and lettuce, she took Benjamin up on his offer to help. Directing him to pull a container of day-old potato salad and newly cut watermelon chunks from the refrigerator, the man placed everything on a cookie sheet, since she didn't have a tray available. After she got drinks for them and gathered up a quilt, they paraded outside to the silver maple tree in her backyard.

Although the temperature of the day hadn't dropped much yet, the prolific tree provided plenty of cool shade as they settled onto the blanket. The slight breeze that whispered beneath its limbs was a welcome addition as well. Before removing their plates from the cookie sheet, they bowed their heads in silent prayer. Guiltily, she had a hard time concentrating. Instead, she found herself wishing she'd grabbed a larger quilt to share with her good-looking neighbor.

In an instant, she realized Benjamin probably hadn't eaten all day. Or at least it seemed that way as he eagerly took one bite after another of his burger. When it was half gone, he stopped long enough to eat a few forkfuls of potato salad. Wiping his mouth with a napkin, he finally spoke. "I know I said the same thing last evening when you cooked for Emma and me, but I'll say it again. You make the most amazing potato salad that I've ever tasted."

Even though she'd heard his similar compliment before,

she still flushed. She was happy that she could please him. *"Danke,"* she said, tasting some of it herself.

Finishing up the potato salad he claimed to love so much, he began to stab at a piece of watermelon then stopped. "I'm glad the *kinner*'s mothers were kind to you today."

The picnic had been tiring in many ways for her. It hadn't been easy being so exposed and looking each woman in the eye, talking about herself. Overall, however, it had been worth the results. She'd gone there wanting Emma to be embraced by the community, and the child's well-being to be considered. Fortunately, being the wise woman that Hannah was, she had steered the women in that direction. First and foremost, as mothers, they'd had a change of heart. As for herself, even though the gathering had brought her closer to the women's circle, she still wasn't in it, no matter how nice they'd all been. But that was fine so long as they wanted what she did—the very best for Emma.

"Jah. Like I said earlier, the ladies showed signs of being more accepting of the arrangement and even seemed to want to be helpful," she answered him. "Which is *gut.* You and Emma deserve their support."

"And you do, too, Miriam." Benjamin sounded beyond sincere. "You're an amazing person."

"First my potato salad is amazing. And now me? Sounds like you're stuck on that word, Benjamin."

She chuckled even though her cheeks felt hot. No one had ever come close to calling her such a thing before. Trying to ignore the sensation, she took another bite of her burger, but not so daintily. A glob of mayonnaise mixed with tomato juice began to trickle down the side of her mouth. Embarrassed, she glanced around the quilt, hoping to spy her napkin quickly. But before she could, Benjamin took notice. He leaned forward to come to her assistance with a napkin in his hand. Oh, no, her heart lurched. Deciding to take care of matters herself, she grabbed the napkin gruffly from his hand.

"You know, you can open up and let people help you sometimes," he said softly.

If only he knew how much she wanted his help and relished his attention. But she feared even his slightest touch could leave her awkwardly breathless.

"Hey, I let you help me with kitchen repairs, didn't I?" she quipped.

"You know what I mean." He tilted his head at her, caring shining in his eyes.

"Honestly, I had a really hard time opening up to Hannah and the others today, but you would've been proud of me."

His forehead creased. Then he ducked his chin for a moment before looking back up at her. "I've really put you in an awkward position, haven't I?"

"*Nee*, I put myself there, Benjamin. Remember?" She gave him a slight smile. Then she cleared her throat and, hopefully, the air between them. "Speaking of help, how was your day at the restaurant? Has Jeremiah been doing a *gut* job? Did you get a lot done?"

He nodded, taking his last bite of potato salad before elaborating. "The place has all been freshly painted. The floors have been sanded and varnished. New chairs have arrived, along with the cash register system I ordered. The deep-vat fryers have shipped and will be here from Cincinnati soon. I should be ready to open the doors in the next several weeks."

"Benjamin, that's *wunderbaar*!" She was so thrilled for him, she had to clench her hands into fists to keep from throwing her arms around him in celebration.

"*Jah*, it is." But even as he said the words, surprisingly, he barely smiled. There was no hint of excitement in his voice.

Unable to help herself, she probed. "Are you getting jitters about the grand opening? It wouldn't be strange if you were," she said, attempting to comfort him. "Why, every year when the new school year starts, my stomach gets to fluttering for days. And that's even after I've been doing the job for many, many years, as you've pointed out recently." She sought to make a joke. He barely reacted.

"*Jah*, maybe I'm a little anxious." All at once he looked past her. Examining her plate, he dodged her further attempts at conversation. "Are you going to eat those last bites of watermelon?"

"*Nee*, I'm full. They're all yours."

As he ate the fruit, she could feel her heart ache, seeing the sudden look of malaise shadowing his face.

"Benjamin? What's wrong?" She laid a hand on his arm.

He finally met her gaze. Placing a hand over hers, he asked, "Want to go for a walk?"

To her, the question seemed to come out of the blue. Helpless to imagine what was going on in his mind, what could she do but answer yes?

Benjamin had asked Miriam if she wanted to take a walk mostly because he needed to get some air. That probably would've sounded ridiculous if he'd said so since they were already sitting outside. But the gentle breeze that was present during their meal had disappeared. Once Miriam had reached out and touched him, the atmosphere suddenly felt heavy. As heavy as his heart.

After depositing their empty plates and her quilt on her back doorstep, they ambled side by side along the edge of her backyard nearest his house. He was thankful for

Miriam's presence and her silence. He knew it was prob-ably difficult for her to keep quiet and not to prod. He also knew he had to explain himself, whether he wanted to or not. Plucking a leaf from the limb of a nearby shrub, he let his feet come to a stop. She halted, too, staring at him.

"I've read that *Gott* has made every leaf unique." He twirled the green stem of the leaf between his thumb and forefinger. "They say there aren't two leaves in this whole world that are the same. And there never have been."

The right side of Miriam's mouth rose slightly. "So I've heard," she said quietly. "It's overwhelming to think about, ain't so?"

"*Jah*, it is." He swallowed hard, realizing what he had to say next. "Miriam, last week I told you that I'd never hold back from you about anything again."

Suddenly the gleam he'd been seeing earlier in her beau-tiful deep blue eyes evaporated. He shifted on his feet as he watched her purse her lips.

"You did say that." She nodded, eyeing him warily. "You *promised* me." She stressed the word.

Dropping the leaf, he reached out, loosely clasping her hand in his. "Miriam, I was saying that about the leaf be-cause a lot of folks think all Amish people are the same. But we're not. At least, I'm not. I'm unique too. But not in a good way, I'm afraid."

Miriam's only response was a perplexed look, and right-fully so. He couldn't hedge any longer. "Roy Caldwell came by the restaurant this afternoon," he said solemnly.

"Oh, Benjamin!" Tenderness instantly resonated in her voice. He felt the caring in her touch as she squeezed his hand as if wanting to console and protect him.

"The moment I saw him, Miriam, I… I hated him," he admitted, his temper rising again.

"I don't understand." Her brow creased. "Why would he come by?"

He paused and sucked in a deep breath, hoping to dissipate his anger so he could explain calmly. Yet he found himself speaking through clenched teeth. "He said he wanted to thank me for not making Ethan's life harder. He offered to help pay for expenses at the restaurant to show his gratitude. He was trying to be nice. I know he was. But it was all I could do to keep from pushing him right out the door." Ashamed, he shook his head at himself. "Miriam, I'm telling you, I want to be a good person. I want to be forgiving and compassionate like all the other Amish folks I know. But I've found that I'm not made like them. When I saw Ethan at Beachy's in his baseball uniform—"

"Is that what happened the day you brought Bumper home?" she interrupted. "I knew something was wrong with you."

"*Jah*, seeing Ethan living his life…" His voice rose and his jaws clamped together so tightly it was hard to say more. Until all at once he realized he was gripping Miriam's hand so hard it could be causing her pain. He loosened his grasp and apologized. "Miriam, I'm *verra* sorry."

"It's fine, Benjamin. It's fine," she said soothingly. "I'm just sorry this is happening to you."

Her hushed tone did pacify him some. Still, it was a minute before he shared more. "Day and night, I keep reminding myself that what happened was an accident. And I know that boy meant no harm. But I also can't help being angry. And you don't have to tell me because I know it's true. I have to get past this—if not for me, then for Emma. If she's meant to stay here in Sugarcreek, it's not fair for her growing up and inheriting these ill feelings for the Caldwells that I have. It's not right at all."

Her eyes were glimmering with tears when she looked at him. He was sure she could see his eyes misting too.

"Oh, Benjamin. There you go, thinking of your niece again, because that's who you are. You've got a good heart. You truly do." She gazed up at him. "But you're not perfect. None of us are."

As she freed her hand from his, he decided maybe she'd had enough of him. But he'd thought wrong. Stepping closer, she wrapped her arms around him, burying her head in his chest, consolingly. Every taut muscle in every limb relaxed. The tightness in his chest eased. The undeniable affection he'd been feeling for her welled up inside him, and he embraced her, holding her as close as he possibly could. Gently laying his cheek atop her *kapp*, he whispered her name.

"Miriam, I'll try harder. I'll pray harder. I'll beg *Gott* for His forgiveness and His guidance so I can forgive others."

She lifted her head and met his gaze. "You don't have to tell me that, Benjamin. I already know you will. That's the kind of unique man you are."

"I don't know what I'd do without your help, Miriam."

"If you only knew how you're helping me, too, by sharing with me." Her voice trembled. "I can't believe I'm saying this, because I've never admitted it to anyone, but for a long while I've done plenty of shaking my fists at *Gott* rather than folding my hands in prayer to thank Him. I've shut out so many people, not wanting to get hurt again."

He didn't have to ask. He knew she was speaking of the father who'd walked out on them. The mother whom she'd had to parent. And others, he was sure, who were put off by her aloofness and hadn't taken the time to get to know her or to understand her pain. A wave of disgust washed over him, knowing he'd lived right next door to her for years, yet he'd been one of those people who hadn't looked past her curtness.

"Can you forgive me for the way I acted?" he asked.

"*Jah*. If you'll forgive me," she said softly.

"And, together, we'll work on forgiving others?"

She nodded as a blissful smile curved her lips.

With the crook of his finger, he lifted her chin higher. Ever so gently, he brushed her cheek with the back of his hand. She was so beautiful, so special to him. He bent his head to kiss her when suddenly the sound of car tires crackling over his gravel driveway reverberated through the air. Jolted, he loosened his hold on her. Instantly, Miriam stepped back.

"Who could that be?" she asked.

"I have no idea," he replied.

Taking her hand, they walked briskly to find out. By the time they reached his driveway, the shiny black sedan they'd heard was already parked and silent, the engine turned off. Looking for a clue, he stared intently. But the front of the car had no license plate and tinted windows hampered him from seeing anyone inside the vehicle. Then, all at once, the driver's door and the front passenger door flew open simultaneously. A man and a woman emerged from the car.

"Stephen?" he exclaimed, completely stupefied. "Angie?" His mouth fell open. His legs turned weak. Blinking from one to the other and back again, he nearly collapsed from shock.

"Yes, we're here! We got back to the States sooner than we expected." His brother approached him with a huge smile on his face and outstretched arms. He gave Benjamin a big, extended, bear hug.

Meanwhile, Angie's singsong voice rang out. "No way we wanted to miss your upcoming wedding. We came a couple of weeks early to visit and help out," she hailed Miriam before locking her arms around her too.

As he and Miriam both stood being caressed by the Bostonians, they traded wide-eyed glances over Stephen and Angie's shoulders. For sure and certain, Benjamin knew he had to appear flabbergasted to Miriam. Because that's exactly how she looked to him.

Chapter Thirteen

Looking in the small mirror atop her bathroom sink the next morning, Miriam wasn't at all shocked to see that the circles under her eyes were nearly as dark as the locks of her hair she was running her brush through. Most definitely, she'd had a rough night of sleep. Make that a night of very little sleep, since she'd tossed and turned in her bed all through the hours of darkness. Considering what an unusually exhilarating and disturbing evening she'd had, of course she'd been restless. Why wouldn't she have lain awake, staring at her moonlit ceiling, wondering what this day, the next week, and the rest of her life, was going to look like?

Oh, how she'd tried so hard to resist Benjamin's closeness! She told herself it was better to back away from him. Yet she was drawn to the sweet man like no other person she'd ever known. No one had ever been so open with her. And there'd never been someone like him that she felt she could be open with too. So when he'd almost kissed her…

Her breath caught as it had the night before. She set aside her brush before she dropped it. Shaking her head of black hair, she tried to shoo away her starry-eyed feelings and steady herself. Yet her efforts were useless. Even as she automatically twisted her hair into a bun and pinned it, her mind continued to wrestle as it had all night long. Her heart thumped wildly as she recalled every sweet second that she'd been in the comforting strength of Benjamin's arms. Just as quickly, her heart turned leaden reliving Stephen and Angie's arrival. What did it all mean? What was going to happen? For sure and certain, they had to tell Benjamin's relatives the truth about the wedding, didn't they? And just as certainly, that could mean the end of her time with Benjamin was drawing near.

Staring at her reflection, she ran a thumb over her cheek, recalling Benjamin's gentle touch. As she did, a gush of sadness welled up inside her. A tear trickled down that same cheek. Even so, knowing what she must do, she swiped it away instantly.

You need to stop this! she commanded her image in the mirror. *No one ever said this pretend courtship was meant to last.*

Forcing herself to take a long, deep breath, she straightened her shoulders. *Whatever happens, you'll survive. You always have,* she reminded her reflection. Yet now, the woman she saw in the mirror wasn't the same person she'd always been. Ever since her time with Benjamin, she'd done more than merely survive, hadn't she?

More conflicted than ever, her unsettledness followed her from the bedroom into the kitchen. Incessant thoughts of Benjamin pulled her toward the window. She stood gazing helplessly at his house. The evening before she'd needed so badly to talk to him and hadn't had a chance to. Once Stephen and Angie had arrived, they hadn't had a moment alone. As they'd all gathered in Benjamin's house, Stephen had talked incessantly about his work, his ideas for Benjamin's restaurant, basically, his thoughts about everything. Meanwhile, between bouts of nodding off, Angie'd kept trying to get Stephen to call it a night so they could head over to the cottage they'd rented. Yet, no doubt about it, Stephen was a big talker. Eventually, when the clock neared midnight, Miriam became worn out as well. Briefly interrupting his monologue, she bid everyone goodnight before heading home.

As much as she wished she could go running next door now, there was no reason to. Benjamin had arranged to meet Jeremiah at the restaurant at the crack of dawn. They had some matters to take care of before the electrician was scheduled to arrive to tackle wiring issues. That's why when Stephen and Angie had suggested meeting for breakfast. Benjamin had pushed them back to brunch. The plan was for Miriam to meet them all at the Corner Café, with Emma, around ten thirty.

Although she loved the Corner Café, Miriam doubted she'd be eating much. Her stomach had been in a turmoil ever since Stephen and Angie had shown up. A cup of chamomile tea did sound soothing, though. Moving away from the window, she picked up the teakettle from her stove top. As she began to fill it with water, a knock sounded at her front door.

Could it be Benjamin? Had he canceled the electrician and come back? Her pulse pounding hopefully, she set the kettle on the countertop and headed for the screen door.

As soon as she saw the person on the other side of her entrance, she froze. There was no hiding her surprise when she opened the door.

"*Mamm?*"

"*Jah*, it's me," her mother clucked.

"What are you—" Miriam blinked. "I mean I'm *verra* surprised to see you." She couldn't remember the last time her mother had visited her former homestead.

"This may surprise you too." Her *mamm* handed her a tin. "I baked sugar cookies for you."

"For me?" Puzzled, Miriam felt her forehead scrunch as she accepted the rare treat.

"*Jah,* for you. Didn't I just say that?" her mother quipped. She paused for a second before asking, "May I come in?"

"You may. It's just that—"

"You're busy?"

"I am," Miriam answered tersely. Mostly, she was in no mood to deal with her mother, of all people. But she couldn't be completely rude. "I have to leave soon," she said vaguely, purposefully not elaborating on what "soon" meant.

"What I have to say won't take long," her mother assured her as she glided inside and took a seat in the living room's worn olive-colored armchair. Squeezing the arms of the chair with her hands, she looked straight at Miriam. "I sat here often, didn't I?"

"*Jah*, you did." The same blue-and-white star quilt had hung over the back of the chair for decades. It was almost that long ago that Miriam recalled her mother perched there staring out the window, hour after hour. Back then, Miriam had taken it for granted that her mother was watching and waiting for their father to come home. Isn't that what Miriam had done from her own bedroom window for so many years?

"Is everything *oll recht, Mamm*?" Miriam set the cookie container on the coffee table.

"*Nee*, it's not."

Miriam sighed, far too worn out for her mother's dramatics. She sank down into a chair across from her. "Anything I can do to help?" she asked politely even though she feared her mother would answer yes.

"You can listen to me."

Miriam's eyes widened at her mother's clipped tone. She prayed for patience before answering, "I'm all ears."

"*Gut.* Because I heard all about the picnic you went to at Hannah Burkholder's. Rebecca told me."

"But Rebecca wasn't there." Miriam frowned.

"*Nee*, she wasn't. She'd been invited, but she couldn't make it since Aaron had a cold. Amanda told her all about it, though. She said there was a lot of talk about the real reason behind your courtship with Benjamin."

Immediately, Miriam tensed. She'd been so wrapped up in her own life, she hadn't thought about how word would get back to Rebecca by way of Jeremiah's sister. Nor had she considered that information would very easily transfer to her mother. It was more irritation she didn't presently need.

"Look, *Mamm*, if you're coming here to say that you told me so—"

"Told you so, what?" Her mother's eyes narrowed, appearing sincerely confused, which was hard to believe.

"From the beginning at Aaron's birthday party, you warned me that there'd never be a future for me and Benjamin. And if this visit of yours is so you can repeat yourself…then I…" she stammered. "I'm not in the mood for this today, *Mamm*. I'm really not."

"You may be a teacher, but you don't know everything, dear Miriam," her mother said, crossing her hands in her lap. "I came here to say I'm sorry, and that you've been an inspiration to me."

Had she heard right? Dumbfounded, her mother had rendered her speechless.

"I've already gotten wind from plenty of ladies who have seen you and Benjamin together, that your fondness for each other looks as real as can be, no matter how your courtship started out," her mother continued. "And, I know you're not like me in many ways, but when your father went away, I believe his leaving left us with something in common. That is, the fear of being hurt again. But since you've been seeing Benjamin, I, uh…" She paused. Miriam had never seen her mother fiddle with her hands so much or be slow to speak outwardly about whatever was on her mind. Finally, she finished her sentence. "I've been spending a lot of time with Marvin."

"Jeremiah's father?" Miriam gaped even though she shouldn't have been surprised. The widower and her mother were around the same age. And she'd heard from Rebecca that Marvin was at their house often, doing repairs. Apparently, that's not all the gray-haired man was working on fixing. A smile twitched at her lips. "*Mamm*, it's been a long time since *Daed* has been gone. I'm glad you found someone you enjoy being with."

"Me too." Her mother grinned. "But I have to say, this relationship situation has gotten me baking more, that's for sure. We've been going on a lot of buggy rides too." She flushed.

"*Gut* for you, *Mamm*," she said sincerely. "I'm sure it's *gut* for Marvin too."

"But that's not all I came here to tell you, *dochder.*"

"*Nee?*" Not sure what to expect next, Miriam braced herself. Following her mother's earlier body language, she also squeezed the arms of her chair.

"At first, I thought Benjamin being such a handsome, likable catch like your *daed* scared me that you'd get hurt. Not only that, but when your *daed* was a young man, he spent a lot of time away from Sugarcreek, too, in the *Englisch* world. Even when he returned here and we married, he talked happily about the experiences he'd had. I really shouldn't have been surprised when he left us to return to that way of living. But…" She leaned forward slightly. "I also shouldn't have projected your father's actions onto Benjamin. That was wrong of me. Plus, Miriam, you're a *verra* special person," her mother said softly. "And I think I've always been a little jealous of you."

"*Mamm*, that's *verrickt.*"

"Not really. I could never be like you. I've been too selfish. But not you. You've taught so many *kinner* for so many years. And now, what you're doing for Emma Byler is so *wunderbaar.* And what you did for our family…" Her voice drifted momentarily. "Your sister reminds me quite often that you were more of a mother to her than I ever was." She rubbed the palms of her hands on the skirt of her dress. With a pinched forehead, she eyed Miriam, looking anxious as to how Miriam might respond.

"Rebecca says that?" Miriam winced. "She shouldn't. You…you did the best you could, *Mamm.*"

All at once, the truth of that statement struck her deeply. In all the years that had gone by, how had she never realized that her mother truly hadn't been able to do better? Her mother had chosen to keep drowning in self-pity for the longest while, as if that was all she was capable of.

Reaching for the tin of cookies, Miriam opened it and offered some to her mother as an unspoken truce. Then she began asking questions about Marvin and recipes. After sharing lighthearted conversation and the sweets, Miriam noticed that, as her mother rose to leave, her face appeared smoother and less lined than when she'd first walked in.

As Miriam stood on her porch, watching her mother get into her buggy, she made a vow to herself. Her mother would never know how much it had hurt her to lose her father and then her mother too. Or how painful it'd been to have her own childhood taken away from her in so many ways.

If, and when, those feelings arose again, she'd offer them up to the Lord above. Because last evening she'd promised *Gott*, Benjamin and herself that she wasn't looking backward anymore. She needed to move forward, no matter what degree of forgiveness, self-constraint and openness that might require of her.

Oh, Benjamin! I pray I can do that without you if I have to. Her thoughts turned to him as she gazed upon his empty house next door. *I let you into my life! And, oh, how the loving strength of you has softened me!*

Nearly a half hour later, Miriam stood alongside Hannah in Benjamin's front yard, watching Emma, Sarah and the twins romp around the grassy field of his property with Bumper. All four of the children had been excited to retrieve the kid goat from its home in the barn the moment they had arrived. She was glad they had the perfect activity to keep them busy until it was time for her and Emma to head into town to have brunch with Benjamin and his brother and sister-in-law.

She only wished she had something to distract her from the jumble of thoughts swirling around in her head. Her stomach tightened for the umpteenth time that morning, dreading meeting up with Stephen and Angie for brunch. For sure and certain, it had been nice of them to drive all the way from Boston to want to be a part of the wedding preparations and celebration. The celebration that wouldn't come to pass. But even so, she wished they hadn't come at all. Or wouldn't have come so soon. But why even think that way? So she could have any more time to fall even deeper in love with Benjamin?

Love!

She shifted on her feet and covered her hand over her

mouth, wondering if she'd gasped out loud at the realization. Hannah must've noticed something because her friend was staring at her.

"So, are you going to tell me what's going on?" Hannah asked softly. "Or do you want me to guess?"

Miriam looked at her new friend, flummoxed. "Why do you think something's going on?"

"The dark circles under your eyes are one clue. And you've seemed mighty lost in thought ever since we arrived." Hannah raised her chin, looking straight into Miriam's eyes. "Also, I couldn't help but notice the way you hugged Emma like you hadn't seen her in forever and may never see her again."

Hannah's perception of everything she was feeling couldn't have been more accurate. At once, Miriam wrapped her arms around her chest as if she could shield herself from the emotions that had been welling up inside her for hours. But hard as she tried, she couldn't stop those feelings from erupting. Tears streamed from her eyes. And choked her words. "The courtship…it may be…it may be over with Benjamin."

"What?" Hannah's voice sounded as piercing as the stabbing in Miriam's heart. "I just saw you yesterday. How could that be?"

"It's…a long story." Miriam lifted the frame of her glasses, bent on wiping away tears and getting a hold of herself. No way did she want Emma or any of the children to see her so upset. Unfortunately, her attempt was useless. The droplets kept coming.

"I'm here to listen." Hannah placed a caring arm around her shoulders. "Unless you don't want to tell me."

Hannah's kindness gave rise to even more emotions. Miriam's thoughts clashed, thinking she should remain silent and keep matters private. But how was she going to manage sitting across from Stephen and Angie and eating if she couldn't relieve some of the angst inside her? Wasn't sweet Hannah the perfect person for *Gott* to send into her life at this moment?

"Maybe we should go sit on the stoop." She sniffed, pointing to Benjamin's front porch steps.

Hannah hugged her around her shoulders all the way to the staircase. Once they sat down, Miriam took a deep breath.

"I'm sorry to break down on you that way," she apologized.

"It was me who invited you to." Hannah offered a wistful smile.

Gratefulness rose in Miriam's chest. "You remind me of Lizzie."

"I'll take that as a compliment." Hannah truly appeared pleased. "So…" she hedged. "Did you and Benjamin have an argument? Because couples do argue, you know. Not everyone agrees all the time."

"Oh, *nee*. Nothing like that." She shook her head. "In fact—" Glancing over at the side of her yard, she could feel her cheeks heat, recalling how they'd held one another so tight.

"*Jah?* You were saying?" Hannah's eyes twinkled.

"We shared so much last night. And then…" She shook her head, still not believing what had taken place. It was all so precious. "It seemed Benjamin was just about to kiss me when a car pulled into the driveway. It was his brother Stephen with his wife Angie."

Hannah's eyes shot open wider. "They were coming to take Emma? But they can't!" she exclaimed, sitting straighter.

Miriam laid a hand on her friend's arm. "*Nee*, Hannah,

they weren't coming for Emma at all. Or, at least, that wasn't their plan, but that may happen in the end. Because they came to town so they could be here for our wedding."

"Your wedding?" Hannah's face lit up. "You never said anything to me, but I'm so thrilled for you, Miriam. I truly am."

"Don't be. It's the wedding Benjamin had lied to his brother about a while ago, so Emma could stay here. The wedding that's supposed to be happening in two weeks."

"Oh, now I get it! *That* wedding!" Hannah's eyes were still sparkling. A grin as wide as her face revealed how tickled she was. Meanwhile, Miriam couldn't share her friend's pleasure.

"Hannah, you've been such a dear friend to me, but I don't think you understand. Since our courtship was all pretend, there is no engagement. There are no wedding plans. When the truth comes out, no doubt it will be the end of Benjamin and me."

Hannah squeezed her hand consolingly. She finally seemed to hear what Miriam was saying. Somewhat. "But if Benjamin was about to kiss you last night…"

"I could be wrong about that."

"But what if you aren't?" Hannah asked. "What if everything happening between you two isn't all pretend?"

For Miriam, that was a huge what-if. Honestly, it was the question that had kept her awake most of the night. Sadly, the answer wasn't hers to give.

Chapter Fourteen

❧

At a quarter after ten, when the electrician was just getting started rewiring the restaurant, Benjamin approached Jeremiah. "Hey, I've got to run out. Do you mind being in charge until I get back?"

"*Nee,* not a problem. Take all the time you want."

Benjamin thanked him, although halfheartedly. As much as he loved his brother and sister-in-law, he was anxious about being in their company, fearing what questions might arise. He'd much rather be in Jeremiah's shoes and staying at the restaurant working.

Despite that the brunch wasn't exactly something he was looking forward to, Benjamin wasn't about to be late for it. Especially for Miriam's sake. Leaving Joy and his buggy parked at his unfinished restaurant, he decided to make his way to the Corner Café by foot. The distance between his up-and-coming eatery and the established café wasn't too far. It was an easy walk, and he needed to get some air. He frowned as that thought shook him. Hadn't he been feeling like that a lot recently?

Yet the summer atmosphere was anything but refreshing. Laden with humidity and lacking even the slightest breeze, the air felt weighty as he strode down the sidewalk. But then, it was the perfect fit for the heaviness he'd been dealing with ever since last evening and all through the night. Even though he should've gone to Miriam's to talk to her after Stephen and Angie had left, he hadn't. He'd told himself he didn't want to disturb her and that she needed her sleep. So then why hadn't he stopped over to her house this morning before leaving for work?

You know why.

Catching a glimpse of himself in the window of the Village Market, he stopped and scowled at his image.

You didn't go because you're a coward. You don't want your brother to know the truth. And you don't want Miriam to know the truth about how you feel. You don't even want to know yourself. Because either of those ways could mean the end of your courtship with Miriam. Maybe even keeping Emma too.

Without a doubt, he realized that just because Miriam had comforted him the evening before didn't mean her feelings ran as deeply as his. He'd seen her comfort Emma in plenty of ways, plenty of times. Maybe she'd done the same for her sister and mother too. And that? That *was* the truth. Besides, back in Cincinnati, hadn't he mistaken the intensity of Megan's feelings for him? She'd even spoken of love right before discarding him from her life.

He sighed before picking up his pace again.

In a matter of minutes, he opened the door to the café. A hostess warmly greeted him.

"Are you dining alone?" she asked.

"*Nee.* I see my group over there." He pointed to a section of booths on the right side of the restaurant. In one of them, Stephen and Angie were already seated on one side of the booth, while Miriam and Emma were seated on the other.

As he neared their table, his eyes caught hold of Emma's body language, and his gut wrenched. Snuggled into Miriam's side, she looked wary and every bit as shy and uneasy as she'd been months ago.

Then, all at once, he remembered his niece hadn't seen Stephen and Angie since the funeral, the most tragic even in her life. Before that horrific event, how often had she seen the pair? As far as he knew, they'd been as absent in her life as he'd been at one time.

Unquestionably, Miriam was the person whom Emma had known the longest. She was also the individual that Emma most likely trusted the most. Even so, when he went to sit next to his niece, her greeting made all the uncertainties of his day momentarily float away. Her blue eyes looked up at him and she hugged him with her smile. He hoped his grin made her feel the same.

"We missed you last night, sweet *maedel*. Did you have a fun sleepover?" he asked.

She nodded wordlessly, but the sparkle that lit her face said it all.

"Gut." He winked at her before addressing everyone else at the table. "Sorry to keep you all waiting. I didn't think I'd be late," he apologized.

"You're not." His brother glanced at the glossy wristwatch on his wrist. "You're right on time."

Angie and Miriam scarcely acknowledged his arrival as they were both concentrating on their menus. He guessed Angie was intensely studying the café's selections since she'd never eaten there. Whereas he had to assume, since Miriam was familiar with the menu, she was probably trying to avoid direct eye contact with him.

"Have you ordered yet?" he asked.

"Nope," his brother answered between thumbing at his cell phone. "But we can, whenever the ladies are ready."

He so desperately wanted to initiate a conversation with

Miriam. Anything to have her look his way. When she finally laid her menu aside, he asked inanely, "Are you getting your usual farmer's omelet, Miriam?"

"Oh, you know me." She gave him a quick glance and a wan smile.

"*Jah,* I *think* I do."

"You know what?" Angie looked up. "I'm going to order the same, Miriam. The farmer's omelet sounds fitting since we're out here in the boonies. I mean out in the country," she rephrased with a chuckle. That decision made, she also set down her menu and began peeking back and forth at him and Miriam.

"You two are so sweet together," she remarked. "I noticed that last night. Now, how long has it been that you've known each other?"

As soon as his sister-in-law posed the question, Benjamin froze. Did she mean how long had they been neighbors? Or how long had they supposedly been smitten with each other? He started to stutter an answer when, thankfully, Miriam spoke up.

"We've known one another since we were *kinner*. Children. So, it feels like forever, I'd say." Miriam paused, appearing to be second-guessing what she'd said. "But not forever in a bad way," she explained. "Forever, in a *gut* way." She pushed her glasses up on her nose, which right away let Benjamin know the level of her discomfort. His insides twisted, regretting putting her in such a position where she had to pretend.

Meanwhile, Angie cooed from across the table. "Aww. How sweet! Stephen, isn't that the sweetest?" She repeated the word.

Stephen shrugged. "The Schrocks always lived next door to us," he replied.

Benjamin was glad Stephen chimed in. It gave him the opportunity to switch the focus to anything other than his and Miriam's relationship. "But as I'm sure you probably already know, Angie, Stephen was the oldest of us Byler boys. So he wasn't around through all of our growing-up years."

"Yes, I'm older by a lot," Stephen replied. "Benjamin is ten years younger than me," he told his wife.

"I know that. You've told me before." Angie frowned. "And I also knew from when we were in town months ago that Miriam lived next door. I just didn't know how long you've lived there, Miriam. That's why I was asking. I was also wondering—"

Benjamin swiftly cut her off, acting as if he hadn't heard her. "And not only was Stephen older, but then I'm sure you also know, Angie, how at sixteen he moved to Cleveland. That resulted in more years that he was away from our family."

"True." Stephen nodded. "But we still have a bond. Ain't so, *bruder*?"

Benjamin smiled, hearing how Stephen not only recalled the Amish phrase, but also used it. "For sure and certain, we do," he answered. "We always will."

He didn't know if he'd ever be as close to Stephen as he'd been with Roman. That stood to reason, since he and Roman were nearer in age and had gone through many of the trials and tribulations of growing up together. Even so, Stephen was kin. They were part of the same family.

Then why hadn't he been able to bring himself to tell Stephen the truth from the very beginning? Why had he gotten them all in a situation that may not have a happy ending?

The answer was right at hand. Everything he'd done was all because of Roman and Lizzie's daughter, his precious niece sitting next to him. Turning to her, he wanted so badly to scoop her up in his arms and protect her. He wanted to safeguard her from anything else that could ever go wrong in her life. But in that moment, the only thing he could do was grin at her freckled face and ask the simplest of questions. "Are you getting the blueberry pancakes you like so much?"

"*Jah*, I am." Emma nodded happily, giving his heart a lilt like always.

Overhearing them, Angie drawled out an "Aww" for the second time. Placing a hand over her heart, she uttered, "How nice, Benjamin. You even know what your niece likes too."

"I try to," he said sincerely. Getting acquainted with Emma and making the child feel loved and whole was at the top of his list now every day of his life.

"He does more than try. Benjamin truly *knows* his niece," Miriam stressed.

The woman he was so besotted with finally gave him a long look. Yet he couldn't exactly read what he saw in her expression-filled eyes. Sorrow? Admiration? Uncertainty? All the above? He couldn't be sure.

After they'd ordered, Stephen got up from the table a few times, excusing himself to take business calls on his cell. Angie easily filled in his brother's void, asking both him and Miriam questions about the Amish. Again, Benjamin was grateful that her curiosity had shifted from their personal lives to their Plain way of living.

Once the food arrived and Stephen had returned to the booth, conversation was more infrequent in between bites of food. When something did come up, somehow Stephen managed to steer the topic so that it pertained to his work. Listening to his brother go on and on, Benjamin vowed to himself and *Gott* that, successful or not, he'd never get so involved in his restaurant. He'd never let his place of work take over his life or take all his attention away from the people he loved. It was a promise he'd happily make to Miriam. Still, his heart sank, wondering why he was even thinking that way. Who even knew if she'd care to hear a pledge like that?

True to form, Stephen ate with as much vigor as he put into his job. The first to finish eating, his brother hopped up from the booth yet again to take another call. Benjamin noticed the rest of them were consuming their food at about the same pace. It gave him great pleasure to watch Emma eat one blueberry at a time and then pour additional syrup on her pancakes. He also noted that, with fork in hand, Angie was toying with the last few bites of her omelet. Miriam must've seen the same.

"It's a lot to eat, isn't it?" Miriam asked his sister-in-law. "I'm getting full myself."

"It's delicious. But, yes, I'm not used to eating so much in one sitting." Angie set down her fork. "Or maybe it's because Stephen and I rarely sit at the table long enough to eat much. Or at least, Stephen doesn't." Angie angled her head toward the spot at the entrance where Stephen was still on his phone. "I admit I've always been married to my job too. That's where Stephen and I met, as you already know. But in the last year or so, I'm beginning to think there might be something else in life besides work. Believe it or not, in the past few months, your brother has been hinting at that too. And the fact is, my biological clock is ticking." She cast her eyes on Emma. "Anyway..." She looked at him. "I'm sorry it's turned out that Stephen has had to work so much on this trip so far," she apologized.

"Don't be," Benjamin replied. "I have to get back to work myself."

"You do?" Miriam blinked at him.

He gulped at her tone of voice. It sounded too much like the Miriam he used to know. And, suddenly, he wondered if all the headway they'd made in their relationship was only in his mind. But then she could probably sense he'd been avoiding her since last night. So, how could he blame her?

"I'm sorry, but I do." His mind flashed to the electrician back at his restaurant. Guiltily, he also reminded himself of the vow he'd made to himself less than a half hour ago. "But I'll be back home early, I promise," he told her.

"So you'll be home a while before Angie and Stephen come over for dinner? Because I really need your help with a few things."

He cringed inwardly, having no doubt what she was talking about. As much as he dreaded it, a talk about how to deal with their so-called upcoming wedding couldn't be put off any longer.

"Benjamin, if you need to keep working, I can come over early to help Miriam," Angie offered.

"*Nee*. No," both he and Miriam answered at once.

"Thank you for offering, Angie, but I can get back to the house in plenty of time." He turned to face the woman who had a hold on his heart. "I promise, Miriam," he repeated purposefully, hoping hearing that from him again would still mean something.

Immediately her gaze met his. His chest tightened as she seemed to be studying him.

Finally she replied, "All right then."

She inclined her head in a small gesture of thanks. But he'd take it and be glad for it. It was the closest he'd felt to her since he'd arrived.

With that, he held up his hand to wave for the waitress to bring them their check. Instead two women he recognized approached their table.

"Were you waving at us, Benjamin?" Frieda Klinger teased.

"He was probably waving for us to keep moving on." Clara Kilmer laughed.

"I'd never do that, Clara. You were the one who let us know about Bumper, Emma's favorite family member. Isn't that right?" he asked his niece.

Emma giggled.

"Are you ladies coming or going?" Miriam asked them.

"We just finished eating, and we're headed home," Frieda said. "Clara is off work today."

"Oh, so you both get to work at your houses then." Miriam chuckled.

"*Jah.* Don't you know it." Clara smiled.

Meanwhile, Frieda leaned closer, speaking to his sister-in-law. "You're Stephen's wife, right?"

"Oh. I'm sorry." Benjamin spoke up. "*Jah*, this is Angie," he said. "And, Angie, these two ladies are Frieda and Clara."

"Nice to meet you both." Angie nodded.

"*Danke.* I remember seeing you at—" Frieda halted mid-sentence and flushed.

He was sure Frieda was about to mention how she'd seen Stephen and Angie at the community funeral service for Roman and Lizzie that had been held in Betty and Levi Yoders' barn. Fortunately, she switched gears so that Emma didn't have to be reminded of that day. "How long will you be staying in Sugarcreek?" she asked.

"*Jah.*" Clara jumped in. "How long are you going to be visiting our favorite new couple and sweet Emma?" She laid it on as thick as the molasses his *mamm* use to make. He gave a sideways glace to Miriam, whose ivory complexion had paled to a ghostly hue. Then braced himself.

"Oh, Stephen and I will be here until a day or so after the wedding."

Frieda frowned. "Who's getting married? Do we know them?"

Angie's face contorted. "You're looking right at them. Benjamin and Miriam."

Shock registered on both women's faces. Emma sat up, glancing back and forth at him and Miriam.

Fortunately, or not so fortunately, he wasn't sure which, Frieda's questioning expression turned into a huge smile. "Why, of course! *That* wedding! I must be losing my mind." She circled a finger around her temple.

"With all those *kinner* of yours, why wouldn't your brain be boggled, my friend?" Clara chuckled before attempting to explain to Angie. "I think what Frieda is thinking is that Benjamin and Miriam have been so tight knit, it's like they're already married and have been that way forever."

"Miriam did say they've known each other that long." Angie sighed. "So romantic."

"*Jah, jah.* So true, so true." Frieda mimicked his sister-in-law's wistful look.

Hearing all that was being said, he saw Emma glance at Miriam, whose mouth had dropped open. And it didn't appear to be closing any time soon. Then his niece turned to him and tugged on his sleeve.

"*Onkel* Benjamin, am I getting married with you and Miriam?"

Angie laughed. "Of course, you are, dear child," she blurted. "And what a glorious day it's going to be."

"Oh, *jah,* glorious," Clara chimed in.

"Just *wunderbaar,*" Frieda exclaimed. "And we'll see

you then, Angie, if not before," she said to his sister-in-law prior to grabbing Clara's arm and hustling away.

Not even a minute after the ladies departed, Stephen joined them at the booth again. "Did I miss anything?" he asked.

"Not really." Angie shrugged at her husband. "Nothing you don't already know."

At that point, Benjamin dared to look over at Miriam and found she was staring right back at him. Unfortunately, the stressful lines he'd noticed creasing her forehead appeared deeper than ever before. As for him, he suddenly had an upset stomach. As they all got up to leave, he wished he hadn't eaten all his pancakes and Emma's leftovers too. Yet his overeating wasn't the worst of it. His heart felt like it had sunk into his shoes. He knew he'd keep feeling that way until he set things right with Miriam.

Chapter Fifteen

❧

"Will I have a new dress to wear for the wedding?"

Emma poured two-thirds of a cup of milk into the bowl of strawberry shortcake batter sitting on the kitchen table. Miriam knew the dessert they were making for their dinner with Stephen and Angie was not Emma's focus. Sadly, the girl was bent on finding out more about plans for the wedding. The wedding that was never going to happen.

In most circumstances, Emma's enthusiasm would've been endearing. In this case? It was breaking her heart to pieces. For what seemed like the hundredth time, Miriam bit her trembling lower lip so hard that it hurt. But she had to endure the pain. She had to do whatever she could to not break down—even though she'd come very close to doing just that at breakfast. As much as she had wanted to gaze at Benjamin and try to read what was on his mind, she'd forced herself to barely look at him. Because, in no way, did she want to see the twinkle in his eyes that drew her in like a magnet. Or to catch a glimpse of a smile on his lips that could make the rest of the world fade away. Or even to feel a tug of attraction seeing his ruggedly handsome face.

So, no, she'd steeled herself. She'd shielded her heart. She'd restricted herself to keep going through the motions. That is exactly what she'd done in the past few hours, preparing creamy chicken to bake later before Stephen and Angie's arrival. As well as cubing potatoes to be boiled for mashing, making Benjamin's favorite corn relish and chilling that side dish along with cut strawberries covered with sugar.

And now she needed to do whatever it took to remain on course and keep waves of emotions from taking hold of her in front of Emma. Unfortunately, that included avoiding another one of the sweet girl's wedding questions for what seemed like the hundredth time too.

"For this dessert, we also need four teaspoons of baking powder," Miriam replied matter-of-factly.

That said, she stepped away from the table and automatically opened the cabinet door to the right side of the sink. There she spotted the container of baking powder right where it always was, sitting among the other herbs and spices. But before she could even reach for it, within a millisecond, tears misted her eyes. All the contents of the cabinet blurred.

She'd cooked so many meals in Benjamin's kitchen in the past few months that she knew it as well as her own. She even preferred it to her own. Not because of how it was laid out or because of any utensils there. Rather, in his kitchen, she felt like a part of something. As if she were making memories instead of being haunted by them, as so often happened in her own home.

That was, until now.

Would this be the last dinner, the final dessert, she'd ever make inside this house? Could that really be?

"Want me to help you find the baking powder?"

Emma's voice interrupted the downhearted one reeling in Miriam's head. She swallowed hard and bit back tears. "*Nee, nee.* I've got it."

Grabbing the baking powder, Miriam shut the cabinet

door. Turning, she handed it to Emma, along with a measuring spoon. Yet even counting out the exact number of teaspoons didn't keep Emma's brain from straying to her current favorite topic.

"Will Sarah and the twins be at our wedding?" she asked. "What day will it be? We won't be in school yet, will we?"

This time Miriam bit her upper lip instead of her lower one, working so hard to contain herself before answering. Though ungenuine, she managed a half smile. "You ask a lot of questions, *liebling*."

"I know." Emma added the last teaspoon of powder to the mix. "It's because I'm so excited." The wide grin on her freckled face was proof of that. So was the way her eyes sparkled. "And I want to know everything so I can tell Sarah."

As much as Miriam always cherished every moment she spent with Emma in the kitchen or anywhere, there was no way she could endure being around the child for much longer. It was becoming far too difficult to hold back her tears.

Clearing her throat, she could only hope she sounded normal despite the dull heaviness centered in her chest. "I have a question for you. Isn't it time to feed Bumper?"

Emma glanced at the kitchen clock. "Oh, *jah*. And I need to tell him about the wedding." She gleamed.

Without bothering to take off the apron her mother had sewn for her, Emma went skipping from the kitchen and out the front door. Her joyfulness only amplified the aching in Miriam's heart. She'd been standing strong for so long that her legs finally couldn't hold her up a minute more. Slumping into a kitchen chair, she pushed the bowl of batter away, wishing she could push away everything that was happening as easily too.

"But I can't," she cried out. "I can't!" she echoed. "What

if I'm losing Emma? Losing Benjamin. Losing the only loves that I…"

She'd called out to empty rooms of her own house so many times throughout her life. Yet now, choking on her words, she couldn't finish what she was declaring. Even so, it didn't matter. She'd never loved a man or a child the way she loved Benjamin and Emma. The intense reality of that and of what she might be about to lose was gut-wrenching. Hope withered up inside her, replaced by grief. Burying her head over her crossed arms on the tabletop, the sobs came abruptly. At first from a deep place. But then she yielded to the sobs that shook her entire body.

Miriam didn't know how long it took. But, little by little, her sobs turned to sniffles. Then there were short gasps here and there before calm finally settled over her.

Sitting up, she lifted the skirt of her apron and blotted the wetness from her eyes and cheeks. Silence filled the room while thoughts rattled through her mind.

Oh, how quickly things had changed. Just the evening before, Benjamin had said so much, shared so much. Yet he hadn't come to her late last night or early this morning to talk to her and put her at ease, had he? And what had she done? She'd made excuses for him. If he truly cared for her, wouldn't he have at least done that? And what about now? Was he ever going to show up? She glanced at the clock, seeing that there wasn't much time left before Stephen and Angie's arrival. Was he trying to avoid her all over again? Had seeing Stephen and Angie somehow brought him to his senses?

Get over yourself. He doesn't love you. Don't you see that?

She clutched the fabric of her dress closest to her heart, sickened by the thought. But then, staring out the window, she realized maybe she'd also changed in the hours they'd been apart.

Just this morning, she'd thought about how Benjamin had softened her. Now, she wished she'd never known what wholeheartedly loving the man was all about. And why had she ever thought love would be hers anyway?

She'd been so much better off before, being closed off with people and not being a part of their lives. She needed to shut herself off again, and she would. But she couldn't do it living next door to the only man she ever really, truly, loved. Why, for so long she'd been holding her breath checking her mailbox each day, hoping there'd be no letter from her cousin, hoping this courtship would never end. But now, even if she never heard from Francie, she still needed to move and get far away. Until then, she'd do what she'd done most of her life. She'd put on an act. She'd give a show of staying sturdy and strong.

Determined to do just that, Miriam rose from the chair. Gripping the wooden spoon in her hand, she began stirring the batter, mixing it well. After smoothly spreading the mixture in a baking pan, she made the crumbly streusel topping. Then she sprinkled it on top as evenly as she could. After all, if this was to be her last dessert made in the Byler kitchen, she wanted it to be perfect.

Usually, something like the swirling aromas of chicken baking and potatoes boiling made for a pleasant entrance whenever Benjamin came home. But today he scarcely noticed. He was out of sorts and not happy one bit about getting back to his house later than he intended.

Obviously, Miriam wasn't too pleased about it either. Bent over the kitchen sink washing mixing bowls, she didn't bother to turn and greet him as she usually did. The disappointment was surprisingly acute. He'd come to appreciate and look forward to the sweetness of her welcoming smiles. Lately those smiles and her shining blue eyes had become the perfect reward for a long workday.

"I'm sorry I didn't get home sooner, Miriam," he apologized.

At the sound of his voice, she finally stopped what she was doing. She wiped her hands on a dish towel before swiveling to face him.

Hands on hips, she asked, "Are you sure about that?"

He cringed inwardly, hearing the old familiar bluntness in her tone. "The electrician had an accident at the restaurant," he explained. "He fell from a ladder and hit his head."

Her eyes narrowed, scrutinizing him skeptically.

"You don't believe me?"

"Benjamin, I want to believe you. Trust me, I do."

That made him feel somewhat better. "Well, *gut*, because I'm telling the truth. We had to call an ambulance for him because he didn't come to very quickly."

"Is he *oll recht*?"

"*Jah*, he is." He hedged for a moment. "But are you, Miriam? I care too much about you to see you so distraught."

Instead of granting him the slightest smile over his concern, Miriam gave him a dubious look and furrowed her brows at him even more. Obviously, he should've never said what he was thinking. The way things had been going between them ever since Stephen and Angie had arrived, it was bad timing. But he couldn't help himself. After seeing the stressful look and sadness on her face that morning, and witnessing it again now, all he wanted to do was to take her in his arms and kiss it all away.

But again, from what he was sensing from her, that

would be awful timing too. He was sure of it when she replied.

"Benjamin, stop. Please. We're not here to talk about you or me. We need to talk about Emma."

"Is something wrong with her? She looked fine, right outside by the porch, brushing Bumper."

"Oh, *jah,* she's mighty fine. She was excited to go tell Bumper all about the wedding. She's beside herself happy. Why wouldn't she be? She doesn't know about our fake courtship. She doesn't know there is no real wedding. And, sadly, the wedding is all she's been talking about."

He leaned against the wall and crossed his arms over his chest to sturdy himself. "She has?" Guilt jabbed his stomach.

"*Jah*, she has. We went to the grocery after we left the café. And when we got home, she took a little nap. I think she was worn out from the sleepover. But ever since she's been up and helping me in the kitchen, it's been one question after another about wedding plans."

He heaved a long sigh. Setting his hat on the counter, he ruffled fingers through his hair. "What did you tell her?"

Miriam answered him somewhat caustically. "What did *I* tell *your* niece? I don't think it's my place to tell Emma that there is no wedding, Benjamin. So, I avoided every question she came up with. But I can't keep doing that and neither can you. She needs to be told what's going on. And I started thinking that—" She broke off midsentence.

"Thinking what?" He gritted his teeth, not sure what to expect from Miriam at this point. It was especially difficult since she kept glancing away from him.

"Emma is probably better off to go live in Boston," she stated flatly.

"Emma move to Boston?" His temper flared. "We already talked about that months ago. I thought we had a solution."

"And how is that working out? At least Angie and Stephen are married and not lying about their relationship. They have stability. And Angie sounds as if she's more than ready to raise a child and has been *verra* sweet to Emma. She's even saying your brother wants to focus on something besides his work."

"Then he can get a dog," he huffed.

She moved forward at that and touched his arm. "Think about it, Benjamin. What's going to happen when word gets around town about the wedding? And you know that'll happen quickly. When there is no wedding, how hurt is Emma going to be? And where does that leave us? You can't keep lying to your brother. And aren't we just lying to ourselves?"

"Lying to ourselves? Is that what you really think?"

Without answering, she turned from him. She sank her hands in the dishwater as if their conversation was over. As if a decision had been made.

Exasperated, he stomped out the back door so Emma wouldn't see him. Feeling like a fist was gripped tightly around his heart, questions tormented him. How had their relationship become so strained? How had it all changed in less than a day? Had it always been nothing but pretend to her?

Cloudy conditions had prevailed all day. So he wasn't surprised when a lightning bolt lit up the sky and a thunderclap boomed in response. After that repeated a couple of times, rain came first in steady droplets then at full force. Normally, he would've fled for cover into the house, but he wasn't ready to face Miriam or Emma just yet. Instead, he found shelter under the closest tree, remembering a poem saying how trees lift their leafy arms to pray. His arms felt too heavy to do the same. Instead, he bowed his head in prayer.

"Where is Emma?" Miriam asked as soon as Benjamin trudged into the house, soaking wet. "Wasn't she with you?"

"No." He blinked. "I didn't see her. Didn't she come in when the rain started?"

"*Nee*. I thought she was with you, so I wasn't worried. But I am now. It's still pouring out there."

"She's probably in the barn with Bumper."

Without saying a word to each other, they hurried out the door and scurried over the field together. The last time it'd rained down on them like this, Miriam recalled how she'd been more joyful than she'd ever been in her life. But worried about Emma, fear nudged at her all the way to the barn.

Walking inside the dry space, the only sounds that greeted them were a few neighs from the horses.

"Emma!" Benjamin shouted. "Emma, don't you be hiding from us. Come out here now."

Running to opposite ends of the barn, they searched every corner while shouting her name, calling for Bumper. Frighteningly, there was no trace of either of them.

"I don't understand." Miriam dug her nails into her palms. "Where can she be?"

"Would she go to the swing?" Benjamin asked.

"In the rain? I don't know why she'd do that."

"I'll go look there if you'll search around your house."

They exited the barn so quickly that she slid in a pool of mud. Benjamin caught her and held her hand until they'd crossed the drenched field and then parted ways. Her heart pounded in her chest as she jogged around the outside of her house before slipping inside. Even though it made no sense at all for Emma to be in there with Bumper, she ran through every room.

Upstairs and down, she kept shouting the child's name. Until, finally, there was nowhere else to look. Standing once again in the living area where she'd first started, she cried out one last time.

"Please, Emma, please." She choked on the words.

No answer came and no movement, either, except for Benjamin coming in the front door.

She shook her head as tears slipped down her cheek. With the crook of his finger, he lifted her chin. Droplets from his wet hair skimmed over his intense eyes. "We're going to find her. You hear me? We have to."

His hoarse voice tore at her heart even more. She ground her teeth determinedly and straightened. "We will."

Without another moment's hesitation, he took her hand in his once again. Rushing from her house, they made their way next door. As they stood at the base of the stairs leading up to his porch, Benjamin gripped her shoulders. Over the roar of the rain, he yelled out his plan. "I'm going to ride out on the road and look for Emma."

"Oh, Benjamin." She gasped. "Do you think she—"

"I don't know. You need to stay here in case she comes back."

Dutifully, Miriam nodded as she crossed her arms over her chest. Rain or no rain, she wasn't moving from her spot. But just as Benjamin rushed off to fetch his horse, she thought she saw something toward the end of the gravel drive. She squinted, the sheets of pouring rain and her dripping-wet glasses blurring her vision. But then the image got a bit closer and—

"Benjamin!" she called after him. "Benjamin, come quick!"

Chapter Sixteen

Benjamin had been halfway to the barn when he heard Miriam shout out his name. Halting his steps, he turned and saw her loping down his driveway in her rain-soaked dress. But then the sight of her disappeared behind a row of pine trees that lined the remainder of the drive. Instantly he took off, bounding in her direction.

As soon as his feet hit the gravel pathway, Benjamin saw what Miriam had been running toward. Splashing through puddles, he ran even faster.

"Emma!" He croaked out loud, his raw emotions spilling into the air. Reaching his niece, he dropped to his knees at her feet, alongside Miriam. Prayers of gratitude flowed ceaselessly through his heart, mind and soul.

Looking up at Emma, in contrast she didn't appear one bit joyful to be home. Her grip remained firm on the end of Bumper's leash, which was dangling from the boy who held her prized possession securely in his arms. As soon as Benjamin laid eyes on that person, his entire body jerked involuntarily. He jumped to his feet. Even if the rain hadn't decided to dwindle down to a drizzle just then, he still would've readily recognized his niece's rescuer.

"Ethan." Overwhelmingly shocked, he had to steady himself before he could say more. "I...don't understand."

The teenaged boy visibly gulped. "The road…it was getting flooded," he explained hesitantly. "I knew you'd want her to be safe. Her goat was too scared to move. Too heavy for her. So I pulled my car over and I…" He shrugged sheepishly. "I hope you don't mind."

"Mind?" Miriam stood up and clapped Ethan on the shoulder. "*Danke*, Ethan. *Danke* for bringing Emma back. And this little guy too." She cupped the kid's wet head before turning to Benjamin's niece. "You're mighty drenched, child. Let's get you into dry clothes." Somewhat reluctantly, Emma let go of the leash and took hold of Miriam's outstretched hand. As the two of them walked away and Benjamin was left alone to deal with Ethan, it seemed he had another storm to face. Eyeing the young man before him, he shifted on his feet, trying to get a grip on the tumult of mixed feelings he'd never had to deal with.

"I'll take Bumper from you," he said bluntly. He held out his hands.

"Yes, sir." Ethan obediently deposited the creature into Benjamin's arms. That done, he dipped the brim of his baseball hat, as if saluting Benjamin, before turning to go.

There'd been a time when Benjamin would've been happy to see the Caldwell boy leave and hope to never lay eyes on him again. But he'd pledged not even twenty-four hours earlier that he wanted to set his soul right with *Gott* where Ethan was concerned. He never would've imagined that *Gott* would've brought Ethan standing before him in this way. But He had.

Even so, Benjamin still had many unanswered questions.

"Ethan, wait. Please."

The teenager swiveled around to face him. Everything in his contorted expression displayed his confusion. Maybe even his fear?

"How did you get Emma to come back?" Benjamin asked. "You said something about Bumper?"

"She said Bumper was one of her best friends. She didn't want him to be scared. She wanted him safe."

His niece's thoughtfulness touched Benjamin, but still, he was puzzled. "Did she say why she left?"

"Well…" Ethan tilted his head. His brows pinched, causing him to look as baffled as Benjamin felt. "She said something about not wanting to go to Boston. So, she was going to live with Sarah instead." His voice was more questioning than matter of fact.

"Ah…" Benjamin let go of a long, deep sigh. "That explains it. She overheard our conversation."

Ethan responded with a blank stare but didn't turn to go. That was a good thing because something else had dawned on Benjamin.

"I've been gone from here for years, so I'm wondering…" He paused, not sure how to ask. "How do you know Emma and knew to bring her here?" He didn't recall seeing Ethan's family at the community memorial visit. "Is it just because it's a small town?"

"Sort of. But I…" Ethan dug his hands into the pockets of his athletic shorts. When he looked down at the ground, appearing shameful, Benjamin almost wished he hadn't asked. He hadn't meant to make the boy uncomfortable. After a pause, Ethan's eyes meekly met his. "I'd stopped by here once because I, uh… I wanted to tell you I was sorry. But then I'd see your niece and knew what I'd taken away from her, and…" He shook his head. "I couldn't bring myself to do it." His voice quavered. "But then, I don't know. Lately, I've seen you with Emma places and she seemed to be happier, like she was healing. And, well…" He bit his lip then took in a deep breath before continuing. "Honestly, seeing that in her has been helping me to heal some too."

All at once, Benjamin felt an unmistakable shift in his heart. It seemed as if a wind had gusted through his entire being and blown out every bit of heaviness there. "I'm glad for you, Ethan. And, Ethan…" Now his voice quaked. "Don't feel like you have to say you're sorry anymore, you hear?"

The teenager nodded and wiped at his eyes. Benjamin felt his tearing up too. "How about I get the buggy hitched, and I'll take you to your car?"

"It's okay." Ethan shook his head. "The rain's stopped. I think I want to walk."

"Well then, *danke* again, Ethan." Benjamin freed a hand from his hold on Bumper. He held it out to Ethan. The boy timidly raised his hand to shake it. "Thank you for more than you know," Benjamin said.

"Uh, sure." The boy's left eyebrow rose a fraction, as if somewhat mystified by Benjamin's last remark. Even so, as they released one another's grasp, he gave the slightest smile. Then he started to leave again.

Once more Benjamin couldn't let him. "Ethan," he called out.

The boy turned to face him.

"You might've heard that I'm opening a restaurant in town in a few weeks. If you're interested, I could use someone like you to wait on tables or deliver to-go orders. Maybe you'd even learn to make BBQ wings if you want to."

"Really?" A sparkle instantly lit Ethan's eyes.

"*Jah*, just let me know if that works for you."

"Thank you, Mr. Byler." He smiled broadly. "I will."

The Caldwell boy's step looked light as he made his way down the driveway. Watching him, Benjamin raised his eyes up to *Gott* in praise. As he did, he felt the warmth of Bumper's affection as the kid leaned in closer to the crook of his shoulder.

"Oh, for sure and certain, *Gott* has a way of getting to us, doesn't He, Bumper? And you—" Benjamin nuzzled his nose in the kid's damp fur. "You saved our Emma once again. I'm just wondering, were you really scared? Or were you just acting that way because of your heart for Emma? And because you knew her heart for you?"

He hugged the kid goat closely, but it was a short-lived pleasure. Just then, he stepped aside as Stephen and Angie's car pulled into the driveway.

"Looks like the time has come to make things right once again," he said to Bumper.

He sauntered up to where Stephen had parked near the house. When his brother and sister-in-law exited the car, they both gave him curious once-overs, and rightfully so.

"Man, you look soaking wet," Stephen greeted him. "Who was that who just left? And what are you doing standing there holding a goat in your arms?"

Benjamin didn't know whether to chuckle about what had just taken place. Or to be deeply concerned of what was likely to happen next.

After all that had happened so far, he decided it best to simply trust the Lord.

"It's a long story," he said truthfully. "I'm going to get Bumper dried off and settled, then I'll talk to you inside."

"I understand if you're angry at me for lying to you and Angie, Stephen." Benjamin bowed his head remorsefully as he made the statement to his brother.

For the past half hour or so, Miriam, Angie, and even Emma, had been in the kitchen busily trying to recover what was left of their burned dinner. At the same time, he'd been in the front room of the house with Stephen, explaining all that had taken place concerning Emma and Miriam in the past months. He also apologized for how he'd handled everything in the hope of somehow salvaging the situation with his brother. Given that Stephen only blinked at him in response, and then proceeded to get up from his chair and cross over to the window, didn't seem promising. And Benjamin's heart sank. Though the clamor coming from the kitchen buzzed in his ears, it didn't block out Stephen's heavy silence.

"This is quite the view." Stephen finally spoke.

Somewhat relieved by the sound of his brother's voice, Benjamin got up from the sofa. Crossing the room, he cautiously stood facing the window, hanging back some from Stephen.

"I realize what you were trying to do for Emma's sake, Ben." His brother continued gazing at the scenery. "This place is peaceful and packed with memories. I always loved how big the sky is here. Not like where I live now." Stephen was rambling. "I look at all this beauty and it makes me wonder why I ever left. And remember how we used to slide down that hill out there in cardboard boxes when it snowed?"

"That hill holds lots of memories." Benjamin chuckled. "How could I forget?"

"Are you glad you came back?" Stephen asked.

Benjamin didn't need a second to reflect on that. "*Jah*, I am."

"Seems like it was perfect timing." His brother's tone was thoughtful. "God's perfect timing."

"It was."

With that, Stephen turned from the panes of glass. "Ben,

I could ask what you want me to do. But I don't think it's my place to do anything just yet."

Benjamin frowned. "I'm not sure what you mean."

"I'm talking about this situation you have going on with Miriam. It doesn't sound like you've resolved everything between you two." His brother dipped his head and raised his brows, giving Benjamin his I-know-better-than-you-older-brother look. Benjamin had seen it plenty in his lifetime, but in the case of him and Miriam, it didn't seem to apply.

"I'm pretty sure she's already said no to me. Earlier she said we couldn't keep lying to you. She also wondered if we weren't just lying to ourselves."

"Hmm. It sounds like she was protecting herself and wanted you to tell her it wasn't all a lie. Women do that sort of stuff, you know. At least, Angie does."

"Oh, now *you're* giving me relationship advice?" Benjamin questioned. "All this from the guy who seems more married to his job than to his wife."

"I hate to admit it, but you're right. You and I need to step up our game. Listen harder. Be more loving. Being here reminds me of how *Mamm* and *Daed* practically cooed to each other sometimes."

Remembering, Benjamin's mood shifted at once. "They were quite the pair. Even though as young boys we thought their carrying on that way was yucky." He grinned. "From what I saw, Roman and Lizzie were just as loving."

"So, what about Miriam, Ben?"

"What do you mean?"

"Do you love her?"

"Well, I... I..." Benjamin began to stutter. As he did, he saw Stephen's eyes grow wide as he stared over Benjamin's shoulder.

Benjamin groaned inwardly, realizing what that look

meant. Miriam had to be right behind him. At once, he swung around. His gut twisted into knots seeing her crestfallen face.

"I'm headed home now," Miriam said almost inaudibly. "I need to change and…well, I need to go." She arched a brow and lifted her chin in determined Miriam style. Then she walked out the door.

And possibly out of his life?

Chapter Seventeen

He couldn't say the words. He couldn't say the words. Why had I ever believed he would?

Miriam nearly tripped down the porch steps, wanting to get away as quickly as she could. Once on even ground, her footing was still faulty with half her energy aimed at fighting back tears.

Don't break down. Don't break down.

But I love him. I love him.

It doesn't matter. It's over. Finished. Done.

"Miriam, wait!" Her heart clenched even more at the sound of Benjamin's voice. "Please, Miriam. You can't just leave."

She picked up her pace and kept walking as if she hadn't heard him. But then, knowing he was gaining ground, she began to run. Yet those long legs of his were too much for her trembly gait. Catching up to her, he caught hold of her hand. Pulling her to a halt, she startled when he gently yet masterfully twirled her around. She held her breath as his eyes searched her face.

She shook her head to get out from under his gaze and wriggled her hand from his grasp. "Benjamin, enough. You don't need to keep pretending. I'm sure Stephen knows everything now."

"Pretending? Miriam, I stopped doing that a long time ago. You've got to believe me."

Everything inside her wanted to. But how could she? Attempting to ignore the sincerity in his voice and the longing in his bright blue eyes, she gave a clipped reply. "Oh, *jah*? You could've fooled me."

"But it's true."

Before she knew what was happening, he swept her into his arms as he had the night before. The memory of their near-kiss brought a surge of tears to her eyes. "Benjamin, please, I'm begging you…" she whimpered, pushing her hands against his chest. "I can't take it anymore. Don't hold me in your arms like this when you're planning to walk away again."

"Walk away from us? Why would you say that? Here I am."

"*Nee, nee.* I heard you talking to Stephen. You couldn't find it in your heart to say you love me, and I'll have to live with that. But, please, as much as I love Emma, I can't do this anymore." She looked away from him, not wanting to feel his closeness, not wanting to see the eyes that she had hoped to gaze into for forever.

"Miriam, would you look at me?" His hands may have been strong, but his fingers were ever so soft as he touched her cheek. Unable to resist him, she turned her face. Her eyes met his. "Miriam, I didn't tell Stephen that I love you because the first time I spoke those words out loud, I wanted to say them to you. So, I'm saying them now. I love you, Miriam, with everything inside me. I love you."

She gasped. Had she heard right? "What did you say?"

"I said I love you."

"Since when?"

"When?" He shrugged. "I don't know. Does it matter?

All I know is I've loved you for a long while now. I love how it feels just to be in the same room with you. I love waking up and knowing I'm going to see you. You're the person who can make me laugh and make me look at things seriously too. And I even love when you argue with me."

"You do?" Hearing him speak of everything she'd been feeling, her emotions welled up inside her. Unable to contain herself, tears suddenly streamed down her cheeks. Happy tears. Apparently, from the concerned expression on Benjamin's face, he couldn't tell the difference.

"Miriam, why are you crying? Is it because you don't love me?"

"Oh, *nee*. I love you so, so much."

"You do?" The joy that bubbled up in his voice and shone in his eyes was unmistakable. "May I kiss you, Miriam?"

"*Jah,* oh *jah,*" she replied breathlessly. Nervously, she held up a finger. "One second." She began to remove her glasses. Wouldn't it be far better not to be able to see the town's most popular, handsomest man so clearly?

"Miriam, why are you taking off your glasses? Don't you want to see me?"

"Well, I…" she muttered, reluctant to explain.

"Please keep them on." He took the glasses from her hand and placed them on her nose. "I want you to see me as I am. I know I have flaws, but I promise to be the best man I can for you."

Taking her in his arms, he lightly kissed the tip of her nose. Delicately, he kissed each of her cheeks. Then his lips touched hers. She quivered, savoring every moment of the sweet tenderness of his kiss. When he finally stopped and gazed up at her, she sighed.

"Oh, Ben."

His head jerked slightly. "You just called me Ben. I didn't

think I'd ever hear you say it. I only invited you to call me that the first time I popped over to your house."

She giggled, hugging him around the top of his broad shoulders. "Oh, you know me. Always playing hard to get."

"Not anymore, I hope." He lifted a brow.

"*Nee*, not anymore." She smiled.

"If that's true, what would you say about getting married in two weeks? You know Amish weddings usually only take that long to prepare."

"I would say...*jah, jah*, yes!" The answer came joyfully bursting from her lips he'd just kissed.

Beaming, he took hold of her hand. "Let's go tell everyone."

"I'd like to change into dry clothes first, and you should too." She squeezed droplets of water from the collar of his shirt.

"Are you already bossing me around?"

"Oh, I was, wasn't I? I need to watch that."

He chuckled. "No, you don't, Miriam. Just be you. Be the woman I love."

He tugged on the strings of her *kapp*, drawing her closer. Before she knew it, his lips found their way to hers again. And it was wonderful.

Epilogue

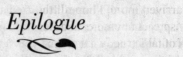

Three weeks later

Danke, Gott, *for another gorgeous day!*

As Benjamin guided Joy over the road toward town, Miriam smiled with wonder as she stared out into Sugarcreek's open sky. Cloudless and with just a hint of a warm breeze, the weather was just the same as it had been a week earlier on the day of her wedding. Her marriage to Benjamin Byler.

Just the thought of it still left her breathless.

She looked over at her husband, always unable to resist the delight looking at him brought her. He must've sensed her gaze. Within seconds, he responded with an affectionate twinkling of his blue eyes and a smile as warm as his kiss.

Not for the first time, she pinched herself to make sure she wasn't dreaming. After all, the wedding had been like a dream, and one she'd never imagined would come true for her.

As soon as their engagement had been announced at worship, the town swiftly came together in every way. Her mother, sister, Hannah, and the mothers of her students had quickly sewed dresses for her, for her attendants, Rebecca and Hannah, and one for a thrilled Emma. Then she was amazed at how rapidly more townsfolk came together to prepare for the ceremony and reception that would last from morning till night for hundreds of expected guests. Stephen and Angie took a true break from work and enthusiastically joined in helping with arrangements. Portable kitchens arrived for cooking all the meals to be served. Tents were spread across her and Benjamin's properties, holding rows of tables and chairs. And the floral centerpieces that graced those tables were beyond lovely.

Yet even with so many folks seeming excited to help, her legs had still trembled as she'd stood with Benjamin before everyone while Bishop Gingerich recited their vows. But once they made those promises to each other, the bishop smiled encouragingly and prayed over them. He'd taken her hand and placed it in Benjamin's, then gently clasped his own steady hand over theirs to seal their vows. All at once, she'd felt calm.

Even seeing her cousin Francie after the service had a soothing effect. Holding up the very letter Miriam had written ages ago, Francie explained why she'd never responded. Apparently, the mail carrier had made a mistake, delivering the letter to Francis King who lived just down the road from Francie. But since Francis'd had his mail on hold during his lengthy stay in Indiana, Francie hadn't received Miriam's letter until King returned to Elizabethtown. That was only a week ago.

"It seems *Gott* knew all along what was best for you, ain't so?" Francie had winked at her.

Peeking at Benjamin once again and at Emma in the back seat of the buggy, Miriam couldn't have agreed more. Sweet thoughts of them both were interrupted, however, when Benjamin spoke up.

"Emma, I think it's time." He glanced over his shoulder at his niece.

"Time for what?" Miriam asked.

"You'll see," he replied.

"She won't see for a while yet," Emma chirped.

"Oh, you're right." Benjamin chuckled.

"You two are making no sense. What are you up to? You're making our lunch date in town sound very mysterious."

Benjamin grinned at her. "It won't be a mystery for long."

And with that, Emma scooted up in the buggy, closer to her, holding a narrow piece of fabric in her hands. "I need to put this blindfold on you," she stated.

"What?" Miriam had no clue what was going on. But figuring it'd be more fun for Emma if she put on an act, she screeched. "You're having me wear a blindfold all the way into town?"

"*Nee*, it hasn't been all the way," Emma countered. "Just now, since we're getting close."

"Well, go ahead." Although happy to acquiesce to whatever was making Emma's face light up, she dramatically rolled her eyes before removing her glasses. She even leaned back a bit so Emma could perform her job. Once the blindfold was in place, she yammered on. "You know, if you two keep ganging up on me like this, I'm going to have to take dire measures. Meaning I won't be making desserts for a week."

Ben moaned and Emma giggled. "I can make desserts for us," she said. "Just like you taught me."

Although blindfolded, Miriam turned to face the child she loved so much. "When did you get so smart?"

"She's had a *gut* teacher," Benjamin quipped. "Ain't so, Emma?"

"*Jah!*" the child squealed.

The jubilant confidence in Emma's voice touched Miriam to the depths of her heart. The three of them had talked, and it'd been decided she'd teach for another year. That would give the community time to appoint another teacher for the following school year. Also, Benjamin had said that she and Emma could come help at the restaurant on Saturdays. They'd be working alongside Jeremiah, Ethan and a few others Benjamin had hired.

"I don't understand," she murmured. "Why am I the only one wearing a blindfold?"

"That's for us to know and for you to find out." Benjamin chuckled.

"How can I find out if I can't see?"

"You ask too many questions." She couldn't see her husband's expression, but she could tell his amused tone.

"Teachers do ask a lot of questions, *Onkel*." Emma defended her, causing Miriam to smile.

With that, they fell into a companionable silence, making Joy's rhythmic clip-clopping more audible and relaxing. Miriam could tell at once when they reached the main street of town. Even so, she had no idea as to exactly where they were headed. When Benjamin finally stopped the buggy, she started to reach to untie the blindfold.

"Nee," he said softly. "Not yet."

Obediently, she sat patiently waiting. Sounds of Benjamin hitching Joy came before he helped Emma down from the buggy. Then, all at once, she felt his closeness. His muscular arms reached around her waist and lifted her from the buggy seat. Once he helped her get her balance, he took one of her hands in his and Emma clasped her other hand. Their combined footsteps sounded on a sidewalk for a couple of yards until they stopped.

"Give me one minute," Benjamin said, letting go of her hand. Meanwhile, Emma still clung on.

Miriam heard him scuffle off, and it was more like two minutes before he arrived back at her side.

"It's time," he said. Reaching behind her, he deftly undid the blindfold. Right away, she saw they were standing in front of his restaurant. The grand opening wasn't scheduled until the weekend. Puzzled, she looked over at him.

"Look up," he instructed her.

She gasped and covered her mouth, eyeing the lit sign. "I thought you were going to call the restaurant the Wing Factory."

"I was. But then I thought Byler's Wings and Rings has a better sound to it, and quite a family history too. It was a dream of Roman and Lizzie's," he said caringly. "It's a place that you might want to own one day, Emma." Miriam watched him and his niece exchange smiles before he continued. "Also, with Stephen and Angie planning to move and work in nearby Columbus, maybe they'll become a part of it, too, somehow. Or at least be frequent visitors." He paused and eyed her thoughtfully. "And then there's you, Miriam." He squeezed her hand. "Miriam Byler, without you, this restaurant would've never come about. You believed in me, and you encouraged me. You've stood by my side."

She couldn't believe her ears. A swell of emotion flooded her heart. Tears welled within her eyes. "I did it because I wanted to. I can't tell you how I…" She swallowed hard. "I've lived in this town my whole life. And so many of those years, it's felt like an empty place to be. And then suddenly you and Emma came into my life, and with you two…it feels like…it finally feels like home to me." She choked on her words. "Oh, there I go again." She wiped at the tears dotting her cheeks.

Benjamin gave her a loving look. "Hmm. The Miriam I used to know never cried so easily," he teased.

"It's *verrickt*, isn't it? What have you done to me, Ben Byler?"

"But your tears are happy ones, right?" Emma asked.

"Oh, my *liebling*." Miriam glanced down at her. "For sure and certain, they are."

"I'm just thankful you opened up and let me in." Benjamin kissed her forehead. "And so grateful *Gott* nudged me into coming to your house that morning."

"I'm so *verra* thankful too."

She uttered an amen to herself then stood on her tiptoes and pressed her lips to her husband's cheek. Then she bent down and kissed the top of Emma's *kapp*. She'd always taught students that one plus one equals two. But in this case? What started out as a pretend courtship between her and the man next door had added up to so much more.

* * * * *

Dear Reader,

You know how sometimes you can't shake something until you get it figured out?

That's how I was with Miriam Schrock. She showed up in my first Love Inspired, *Her Secret Amish Match*, and was there for all of five pages. She was so curt and hard to like that I never imagined I'd hear from her again. But then I couldn't stop thinking about her. Why was she the way she was? There had to be a reason. Because you and I both know when a person is behaving defensively, often they're either scared or hurting, right? Not only have we seen that in others, maybe we've even been there ourselves. So, after unraveling Miriam's past, I set out to make things right and happy for her hurting heart. Of course, I wanted to do the same for Benjamin and Emma too.

I sure delight in being able to pen a character's happy ending. But it's a greater, more awesome joy to know that God is the Divine Author of mine—and of all of ours. That's why I chose the scripture verse that I did. Because in only a dozen words, God says so much. So eloquently, He gives us His promise of abundant hope that we can hold close to our hearts no matter what we're going through. We're assured that His love for us is a story that never ends.

Thank you so much for choosing my third book set in Sugarcreek. I hope you enjoyed it. If you'd like to say hello, I'd love to hear from you. My website is www.cathyliggett.com or please visit me on Facebook.

Blessings now and always,
Cathy